MURDER IN BARE FEET

An enthralling crime mystery full of twists

ROGER SILVERWOOD

Yorkshire Murder Mysteries Book 12

JOFFE BOOKS

Revised edition 2020
Joffe Books, London
www.joffebooks.com

First published 2009

ISBN: 978-1-78931-366-6

CHAPTER 1

Skiptonthorpe High Street, North Yorkshire, UK. 2.00 p.m., Monday, 3 February 2003

Charles Pleasant was every woman's dream of a man. He was 46 but looked nearer 35: he worked out almost every morning, swam, had a massage and then an hour under a lamp almost every afternoon. His body glowed with rude health. Women knew it and women liked it.

He drove his new Range Rover up to the front of Merrill's department store and looked at his watch. He was waiting outside the most expensive store in town for the most important woman in his life, Mrs Bridie Longley. And there she was, struggling through the glass door of the store loaded up with colourful bags and boxes of shopping.

He smiled as he caught sight of her. It always warmed his heart and lightened his life when she appeared. Wherever she went everybody turned to look at her, especially the men, which delighted him. She had those slim tanned long curvy legs that men can't take their eyes off, especially as she wore short skirts from her navel like a cake frill.

But she wasn't smiling. She looked distinctly out of sorts.

He lowered the car window. 'Jump in, darling. We're late.'

She wrinkled her little kitten nose. 'I need six hundred, darling,' she said. She had a warm voice like thick, hot chocolate. 'My card's run dry.'

His jaw tightened then he frowned. 'I put a thousand in on Friday,' he said.

'I know,' she said with an indignant stare. 'But I need another £600. I've seen the most magnificent parasol.'

Pleasant stared at her. 'Parasol?'

'Come on. Come on, darling,' she said like an impatient schoolteacher to a slow pupil. 'Six hundred. That's all. Good heavens!'

He slowly put his hand into his inside pocket and pulled out his wallet. 'I don't think I've got—'

She stamped her feet on the cold pavement and held out a hand. 'Come on, Charles. Don't fool around.'

He pulled out a few twenty-pound notes, but he obviously had nowhere near £600.

'What about your cards, Charles. What about your cards?' She rattled off like a machine gun and then, to soften the outburst, added the word, 'Darling?'

A hot boiling feeling in the lower part of his chest began to work its way upwards. It was raw anger turning into stubbornness. It grew hotter and hotter as it rose up his chest towards his face. He pushed the wallet resolutely back into his pocket and said: 'No, Bridie. I'm sorry. I haven't got it.'

Her eyes grew to double their size and then flashed like lightning. She held the stare in disbelief. Her lips tightened.

'I must have it!' she snapped.

'I haven't got it, Bridie. Now, get in. We're late.'

'Huh! You bastard!' she stormed. She turned round, stared at the shop, hesitated, stamped her foot, then stormed round to the other side of the Range Rover, pushed in the bags and boxes of shopping she had been carrying and then bounced into the seat and slammed the car door.

Her face was red; her hands were shaking. 'You can go to the bank and get it?' she said.

'No.'

'Yes,' she snapped. 'You must.'

He didn't reply. He started the engine and engaged first gear.

'What is it, Charles,' she continued. 'Are you suddenly poor? Is that what it is?' she said scathingly. 'You told me you had money to burn. That nothing was too much for me. You told me you would cut off your arm rather than let me want for anything.'

He pressed down on the accelerator and pulled into the traffic.

'I need that parasol. It goes with my new summer outfit. It would just set it off right. What's the matter? Don't you want me to look nice when we go out? It would make all the difference to my outfit when we go to Nice. We are going to Nice? Aren't we? That is still on, isn't it?'

Pleasant had to concentrate on the driving, but at the same time he was also trying to think of something to say to Bridie that would settle her down without him actually having to grovel. He was desperately searching for the right turn of phrase. He knew it wasn't easy saying no to her. She had such a powerful will, and was, of course, married and he was well aware that she could withdraw her favours anytime, and return to living with husband, Larry. But he also knew that that would not suit her. Her husband was not like most men. For one thing, he had a natural need for quietness, gentleness and peace. That didn't suit her. In addition, Pleasant recalled the repeated disappointments she told him that she had tolerated. The thought of what she had said gave him some confidence in what he must say to her. The time had come. He would have to speak up now, before she bled him dry. At the same time he sighed when he thought how he would struggle to live without her. His entire life had been transformed unbelievably since they became lovers. He could not possibly endure life without her. The emptiness he did not bear to think about. It was not too strong to say that he could not live without her. There was nobody like Bridie Longley. Nobody.

'Are you listening to me, Charles?'

'I hear you, darling,' he said.

'Don't you *dare* call me darling,' she said. 'Not when you are so mean to me.'

He changed gear. His hand so easily could have slipped on to her legs and caressed them, as it had done so many times before. In this mood, she would have rejected such an advance. He simply could not stand the risk of being held at arm's length, like this. The trouble was she knew that too.

'Are you trying to find a hole in the wall, a cash machine?'

'No. I'm trying to find a way through this traffic and get home.'

'Not to your house, Charles,' she said quietly. But it was highly significant. 'Take me home.'

She meant her own home with husband, Larry Longley. It was like a sword thrust into his belly. He would need her tonight. Even one night without her close to him, to put his arms round was impossible to contemplate. 'No need to make a big thing out of this, Bridie,' he said. 'You know I'm crackers about you.'

'That's why you deny me a parasol. The most beautiful parasol I have ever seen.'

'It's not the parasol. It's the principle.'

'It's not the principle, it's the money.'

There was hesitation. He swallowed hard. 'All right, it's the money. I can't afford your spending any more, Bridie. A couple of hundred a week, maybe I can manage, but you're spending over a thousand.'

'You told me you had millions. You're just a tight-fisted meanie. Or a liar.'

'No. Be reasonable.'

'Reasonable,' she screamed. 'You've all those lorries and that big house.'

'It's all mortgaged, Bridie. I've a loan so big, I daren't even think about.'

Her jaw dropped open. 'Huh! You've lied to me.'

His eye was on the road. It was a tricky moment. He carefully contrived to overtake a bus. He put his right foot down and roared ahead.

'What?' he said.

'You've lied to me,' she said. 'You told me you had millions. Have I wasted eight years on you?'

'Money is a bit tight, just now. That's all. Come back to my house, now. I can make it up to you, darling. You know that.'

She put both hands to her head. 'No,' she said. It was going to be a great wrench. She would need great willpower to push him away from her. Larry would be a very poor substitute. No substitute. He was pathetic. 'This has all been a great shock to me,' she said. 'I have to think things out.'

'You're at that time in your life when you need me. You know that.'

It was true. He knew her better than she knew herself.

'I don't know,' she said.

'We have that magic that millions of people wished they had. Don't throw it away because of some trivial thing like … a parasol.'

He saw a 30 mph speed restriction sign. He eased off the accelerator.

'When you think quietly about it,' he continued, 'you'll get it into perspective. Let's go back to my house. You know I can give you a super time. We are always great together.'

'I don't know.'

'We can sort something out about the parasol.'

'It's not only about the parasol, now, Charles.'

'I can't live without you, Bridie.'

'Don't be so bloody melodramatic.'

'If you leave me now, to go back to Larry, I won't be able to help myself. I will kill you.'

St George's Road, Bromersley, UK. Midnight 3/4 February 2003

The church clock struck midnight. Fog had dropped on the town like a shroud. There was no moon. Visibility was five metres. Nervous drivers had abandoned their cars and left them at the side of the road. What little traffic there was crawled like noisy, determined, snails. Pedestrians had long since found their destination and were snug in their beds.

A pair of powerful headlights pierced through the fog as a solitary vehicle ground its unhappy way along St George's Road on the outskirts of the town and stopped at a frontage of lock up shops. The vehicle's engine ticked away, sucking in diesel and blowing out dark fumes as the driver pulled on the handbrake. A few seconds later, the driver, in leather jerkin, woolly hat and leather gloves, and carrying a heavy duty rubber-sleeved torch jumped down from the cab. He walked tentatively across the wide pavement towards the shops and flashed the torch erratically up at the fascias. He found the colourful sign of 'Hellman's Family Butchers' repeated across four shopfronts then waved the light searchingly on the imposing entranceway into the shop. There was no sign of life. He flashed the torch around to see if he was being observed. All he could see was grey fog. Everywhere was silent and deserted. He went straight up to the shop door and tried the sneck. It was unlocked. He pushed the door, went straight in and closed it quickly. It was the largest butcher's shop he had ever seen. He flashed the torch on to the huge length of glass and chromium counters, creating crazy reflections and eerie shadows. He made his way to the back of the shop, and flashed the torch rapidly over a dozen spotless, and bare butcher's blocks in turn. On the nearest, he saw the glittering reflection of the blade of a solitary chopper sticking lightly into its surface. He stared at the shining blade. His hands were shaking. His pulse raced. He quickly snatched it off the block, thrust it under his arm and dashed out of the shop.

A1(M) Motorway Cambridgeshire 6 Miles South Of Grantswood Motorway Services. 2.50 a.m., Wednesday, 5 February 2003

It was a bleak winter's night.

AA patrolman Carl Standish was driving northwards on the A1(M) motorway stretch through Cambridgeshire towards the hard standing, midway between the Little Chef restaurant and Grantswood Services. It was pitch black but no fog or mist. So driving wasn't difficult. There had been a slight air frost and unusually Standish had only had one call since reporting on duty four hours earlier. He preferred to be busy, not overwhelmed; a steady flow of jobs made the shift pass more quickly. He had supplied and fitted a new fan belt on an old Nissan and sent the driver happily on his way and was heading for Grantswood Services, the position he had to wait at when not attending members. There was a constant stream of traffic, but it was not heavy and he drove at an easy 40 mph, behind a heavy, articulated GPO van in the nearside lane. He was thinking how much he would enjoy a drink of coffee from his flask when he arrived and parked up at his waiting station, when the vehicle in front of him braked suddenly. His brake lights came on. It squealed to a stop. He braked hard and only just managed to stop four feet away from the back of the pantechnicon. He immediately stabbed the button to put on his flashing amber lights.

He wrinkled his nose and rubbed his chin.

In his mirror, he saw a stream of vehicles' headlights approach from behind, saw their overtaking indicator lights blinking in the night and then observed them roar past. After a few more seconds, he switched off the ignition, grabbed his rubber-covered torch, withdrew his ignition key and made his way up to the front of the GPO wagon. In the wagon's headlights, he could see the uniformed driver with his hands on the rim of an oil drum about four feet high and two feet in diameter. It was standing upright a few feet from the gutter.

'What's happened?' Standish said.

'This ruddy thing. Dangerous standing here. Dropped off the back of a lorry, I reckon. Somebody will be short when they arrive wherever they're going. Lost an 'eadlight glass to it. Give us a hand, mate.'

Standish grabbed the other side and between them they manoeuvred it to the side of the road. It wasn't very heavy. When at the edge, they gave it a final triumphant push on to the grass. It hit the banking with a thud, the lid fell off and a mess of blonde hair covered in blood slithered on to the grass. Standish flashed his torch at the sight. It had an ear and two red staring eyes, and below, grey, skinny shoulders.

The two men gasped.

Standish's arms turned to gooseflesh.

30 Park Street, Bromersley, South Yorkshire. Sunday, 4.35 p.m., 5 August 2007

Summer had arrived. It was hotter than a crematorium chimney on a January afternoon.

'Michael. Michael. Michael! Are you going to cut that lawn then?'

Detective Inspector Michael Angel was enjoying his weekend off. He was in a deckchair in his garden in his shirt-sleeves and shorts with the *Sunday Telegraph* covering his face. His wife, Mary Angel, came through the French windows in white blouse and tennis shorts carrying a tray. 'I've brought you a cup of tea.'

'A beer would have been better.' He slowly dragged the paper away from his face. 'Have you no consideration? Don't you know, I was almost asleep,' he said. 'I was drifting beautifully. You woke me up.'

'I said, are you going to cut the lawn?' Mary said, stressing each word.

'It's too hot,' he said reaching out for the beaker. 'Thank you, love.'

She smiled and sat down beside him. She picked up a magazine and took out a pen from her handbag.

He looked up and took a squinting look at the clear blue sky.

'Beautiful.'

It had been a dreadful summer … all those floods. The sun was a long-awaited relief.

The only sound was the chime of the church clock.

They sipped the tea. He squinted down at the newspaper. In the corner of a page was a big colour photograph of the representation of a man's head in glowing green. The head was the shape of a football. It had thick lips and slit eyes; it had a short fat neck and the whole thing was set on a wooden plinth.

She looked up from the magazine and saw it.

'Whatever's that?' Mary said.

'I don't know,' he said and read out the headline. 'Jade head of Hang Mung Cheng missing.' Then he went on to say, 'It's the life-size representation of him, found in Xingtunanistan, a small, remote country on the northern borders of China, where he was Emperor in 600 BC. Stolen in 2001. It has been traced to London and the Empress of Xingtunanistan, Louise Elizabeth Mung Cheng, has arrived at Heathrow to speak to the Home Secretary to see if he can use his influence to find the jade head and have it returned to Xingtunanistan. It's two thousand years old.'

'Mmm,' Mary said, 'it looks ugly … but a piece of carved jade that age and size must be worth a fortune.'

'Priceless, it says here,' he added, shaking the newspaper. 'Good luck to her, I say. She'll need it.'

They both returned to sipping the tea.

Mary gripped the magazine tightly, then buried her head in it, pen in hand.

Angel turned the page of the newspaper and was scanning the page for interesting items.

Suddenly Mary said: 'What's the capital of Turkey?'

'Ankara,' he said almost without thinking.

'That's it,' she whooped.

He looked up at her with a frown.

She smiled at him. 'It's for a competition.' She made the entry on the magazine page.

He wrinkled his nose. She was always doing pointless competitions.

Then she went on: 'Mmm. Name three soft cheeses.'

'Brie,' he said. He might have known another two, but there was the intruding sound of a mobile phone.

Mary sighed, looked at him and pulled a disagreeable face.

He frowned. 'Might be nothing,' he said as he dipped into his shirt pocket, found the phone, opened it and pressed a button.

'Angel.'

It was Inspector Asquith, duty officer at Bromersley police station. 'Sorry to bother you, Michael. There's a triple nine. Man shot dead on Sebastopol Terrace. In a car. Slumped over the wheel. Outside a scrap metal dealer's.'

Angel leaned forward in the deck chair. 'Right, Alan.'

'I've informed SOCO and Mac. There's patrol car Foxtrot Tango One attending.'

'Right.'

'Have you informed the super?'

'He doesn't want to know. He said direct any CID emergencies to you. He's gone to a champagne reception to mark the opening of new offices of Councillor Potts of Potts Security.'

Angel nodded. 'Hope he enjoys himself,' he said unconvincingly. 'Who rang in?'

'Didn't leave his name. The usual.'

Mary knew from her husband's side of the conversation what the call was about and what was going to happen to the rest of their afternoon. She pulled a face and said, 'Oh really!'

Angel waved a hand at her not to speak.

'Yes, right. I'll deal with it,' he said and closed the phone.

CHAPTER 2

SEBASTOPOL TERRACE BROMERSLEY SOUTH YORKSHIRE, UK. 4.50 P.M., SUNDAY, 5 AUGUST 2007

Sebastopol Terrace was one of four dark, parallel streets consisting of small Victorian terraced houses of identical design, to provide cheap rented accommodation for worker's at the town's coalmine. Today they were mostly owned by the occupiers and their building societies, and provided convenient accommodation for those who wanted to be near employment in the town or close to the bus station from where they could be conveyed to jobs at factories on the outskirts of the town.

The burning August Sunday sun had tempted many of the cramped residents to the parks and countryside; the poorer and older residents stayed inside the tiny rooms to keep cool behind lace curtains and shades, leaving the gloomy quiet streets unusually deserted.

Disturbing the quiet and peace, an ice cream van came rattling round the street corner playing its inane chime of 'half a pound of two-penny rice, half a pound of treacle', unsettling those who had settled into a warm sweaty snooze. It stopped a while, served a small queue of customers then dashed off to another street where the electronic chime was heard again.

Sebastopol Terrace was a cul-de-sac, and at the end on the site where two houses had been demolished after a gas explosion in the seventies, was a scrap dealer's yard enclosed by high steel railings with big iron gates with barbed wire stretched across the top. There was a big sign in white paint on black, attached to the gate. It read: 'Charles Pleasant, scrap metal dealer. Buyer of ferrous and non-ferrous metals. Best prices paid.'

Crowding the open gates of the scrapyard was an assortment of police vehicles. Some of them had blue lights rotating on top of them. A big black Bentley car was positioned across the pavement facing the entrance to the yard. Six police personnel, four in white disposable paper suits, boots and hats, and two in patrol car uniforms, were assembling a small white marquee around it.

Edging ever closer to the scene were about thirty men, women and boys; they stood there, muttering. The men and boys were mostly white, hands in pockets and naked from the waist up, some with blue tattoos. Several wore grubby vests. The women in twos and threes were stood there with fat arms folded, watching as if it was a street entertainment.

Angel turned the BMW round the corner of Sebastopol Terrace, put his foot down on the accelerator and rocked his way along the uneven road up to the big white SOCO van and parked his car behind it. Then he made his way towards the crowd of rubberneckers to get to the centre of the activity. As he pushed his way through, his lips tightened back against his teeth. When he finally arrived at the DO NOT CROSS tape and dodged underneath it, he sighed and leaned over to one of the patrolmen, PC Donohue, and whispered something in his ear.

The policeman nodded knowingly. He turned, took the notebook out of his breast pocket and looked at the nearest of the young men and said, 'Now then son. What's your name and address?'

The young man shrugged, then turned away and kicked an invisible ball casually along the road.

'Did you see what happened?' Donohue said, following behind him.

The young man walked more quickly, then took his hands out of pockets and began to run down the street.

Donohue turned to the next young man. 'And what did you see?'

'Nothing.'

'What's your name, sonny?'

He also shrugged, turned away, took his hands out of his pockets and began to run. Some of the others heard and saw what had taken place and also turned away and began to drift slowly away. Donohue approached a man in his twenties and said, 'Did you see what happened, sir?'

The young man pulled in his stomach, stuck out his chest and with his eyes half closed, looked down at the flagstones and said, 'No. I didn't see nuthin'.'

'Do you know the man?'

'It's old man Pleasant, isn't it?'

'What's his first name?'

The man nodded in the direction of the sign. 'It's up there. Charles Pleasant.'

Donohue nodded. 'You could do an official identification of the body then, for us, down at the station, couldn't you?'

'S'pose.'

'Right. What's your name and address, sir?'

There was a thoughtful pause. The young man shrugged. 'Naw. It's all right,' he muttered, then he turned and walked slowly away. When he was about thirty yards up the road, he also began to run.

Donohue turned back to another group of four. As he approached them, they turned and walked off. The other lookers also walked away.

Angel noticed, caught Donohue's eye, nodded approvingly and turned back to check over the dead man in the driver's seat. There was a spray of blood on the windscreen and an oval hole in the glass, reasonable to assume it was made with a gun. The dead man had dark hair with speckles of grey. Angel thought he might be in his fifties. The hair was sticking up in places, as if it was soaked in brilliantine.

The SOCO team finished securing the marquee, which completely covered the Bentley. It had a flap that was temporarily fastened open with ties to the scrapyard railings. The arrangement provided a shield from prying eyes whilst still permitting the team access, especially convenient when carrying anything. They set up powerful lights inside, and after the SOCO photographer had completed all his work and had withdrawn, Angel went into the marquee.

Dr Mac, the pathologist, was still examining the head and shoulders of the body through the driver's window, which he had apparently found in the lowered position.

Angel pushed up to him. 'What you got, Mac?'

'Nothing very helpful, Michael. Only what you see,' he said, and with a gloved hand, he gently took hold of the dead man's hair, pulled his head upwards and backwards for him to see the face.

Angel had seen plenty of bodies in his time; each one was different. It was never pleasant. In this instance, the mouth was turned down, the eyes fully open, staring as if still alive.

It sent a tingle down his back.

Angel nodded and Mac let go of the head. It flopped as relaxed as a puppet down across the steering wheel.

Angel pursed his lips. He thought that the face was hard, important looking and brutally handsome. The face of a thinking, intelligent man, not necessarily a good man; definitely not the face of a backstreet scrap dealer.

'I have found four bullet holes. Two in the head, then one in the arm and one in the chest. No powder burns, so the gun was fired well back. More than eight or ten feet, probably much further.'

'Can you work out the projectile path?'

He nodded. 'At a rough guess, I'd say they all came from somewhere over there.'

He pointed to a small roadworks site about sixty feet away from the scrapyard gates.

Angel nodded and noted the spot.

'Time of death, Mac?'

'Not long. Not long at all. Minutes. Less than an hour.'

Angel nodded.

'There might be a lot more info when we open the car door.'

A car arrived.

It was DS Gawber. Angel had phoned him to meet him here before he had changed into his suit.

Gawber took in the scene, saw Angel at the marquee entrance and made straight across to him.

'Sorry to drag you out, lad, on a day like this,' Angel said.

'Don't mind, sir. Brother-in-law and his wife for lunch. And their noisy kids. Went on a bit. Glad to get away from them.'

Angel smiled briefly then pointed at the corpse. 'Seems that the driver was coming into these premises. That's why the car is across the pavement at this oblique angle. The gate's probably locked. In which case he would have stopped the car, got out, unlocked the gates, returned to the car, got in it and before he re-started the engine, he got a shower of bullets.'

'A shower, sir?'

'Mac says at least four. The shots came from the general direction of the roadworks site over there.'

Angel walked over to a hole at the side of the road. There was a 'Road up' sign. Eight cones surrounded a hole about four feet square by four feet deep with a black gas pipe with some small apparatus with a dial on it showing. Next to the hole were a concrete mixer and a heap of the earth that had recently been excavated. The small site had red and white barriers and stood surrounded on three sides of it.

He stood on the pavement, looked across at the white marquee over the Bentley, and tried to align himself to where the gunman probably stood.

'About here, Ron?' Angel called.

Gawber looked in both directions then held up two thumbs.

Angel looked downwards. To his right, on the road he saw a cluster of spent handgun shells, and in front of him something that really surprised him. He crouched down and peered at it open mouthed.

Gawber saw that he had spotted something interesting. He went over and looked down to where Angel was looking. 'What is it, sir?'

Angel pointed into the brown and yellow soil. 'A footprint, a footprint of a bare right foot,' he said. 'Our murderer was bare footed.'

The footprint was clear in the small pile of clayey soil. The shape was unmistakable; it was certainly that of a bare right foot, distinctly showing the toes and an impression that included the heel.

The two men looked at each other. It was hard to believe. Neither could find anything to say.

Angel wrinkled his nose. He stood up and looked around him. 'Tape this area off, Ron. This entire street end should have been given crime scene status.'

'We need more men, sir.'

'Aye. Tell that to the super. He's out, being wined and dined.' He pointed to the marquee. 'Tell Don Taylor I want him urgently.'

Angel quickly directed DS Taylor, who was in charge of SOCO at Bromersley, to take an appropriate cast of the foot with plaster of Paris, while Gawber had the end of the cul-de-sac taped off with DO NOT CROSS – CRIME SCENE tape closing off that section of the street.

Angel and Gawber began the important business of the door-to-door. They each took one side of the road up to about ten houses along. This was a job usually allocated to more junior members of the force but was an important part of the investigation. Angel took the side of the street where the road had been excavated and where the footprint and the gun shells had been found.

The end building next door to the scrapyard was an old lumbering place that looked as if it had been a public house many years ago. It had a dusty, lop-sided cardboard sign, black on white, in one of the front downstairs windows. It read: 'Rooms to let'.

Angel pushed his way through the central double doors, which were unlocked, and led up to a counter of shiny aluminium and Formica plastic panels, like a fish and chip shop. The deafening racket of banging drums, raucous shouting and the battering of various stringed instruments blared out from some loudspeaker located behind a door at the end of the hall. The din caused Angel to screw up his face in pain. Opposite the counter was a steep, narrow staircase leading up the stairs.

Angel pressed the illuminated plastic bell push on the counter and heard an electronic ding dong sound somewhere in the back. The place smelled of microwaved fluff and wet dogs drying out in front of a radiator. He looked around at the fading green walls, dark painted woodwork, worn carpet, dark staircase, plastic-faced counter top and wondered why anyone would want to hire a room in that place.

The racket was suddenly turned off and, at the same moment, a small, bald man, skinnier than a Strangeways rat, showing braces over a once white shirt and wearing crumpled trousers, opened the door at the end of the end of the hall, looked surprised, then scurried up the hallway and took up a position behind the counter.

He stared up at Angel with tiny eyes through dusty spectacles, fingered a book on the shelf under the counter, and said, 'Is it for a single, sir?' He spoke in a nervous, high-pitched voice.

Angel sniffed. The man obviously thought he wanted to stay in the place. 'I'm Detective Inspector Angel,' he said quickly.

The man's left eye twitched.

'I'm making inquiries about an incident that happened outside here less than an hour ago. Are you the proprietor?'

The raucous music started again at perhaps even louder volume.

Angel's eyebrows shot up. He blew out an impatient sigh.

The man's jaw muscles tightened, his eyes narrowed; he looked in the direction of the door. His ratty face looked even rattier. He looked back at Angel. 'Yes, Inspector,' he shouted. 'I am the proprietor. Samson Tickle at your service. What sort of an incident?'

'A man was shot dead. At least four gunshots.'

The racket from the other side of the door was making the cobwebby glass lampshade suspended over the counter dance.

'What did you say?' the man called.

'A man shot dead,' Angel bellowed.

Tickle's eyebrows shot up. He looked away at the door, hesitated, then said, 'Just a minute, Inspector, please.' He scurried down the hall to the door. The noise blared more loudly as he opened it. A few seconds later it stopped.

The silence was exquisite.

Angel blew out a sigh.

He heard the little man shout irritably. 'I can't hear myself think, Marcia. For god's sake. I've got a copper out there.'

Some high-pitched female voice screamed something in reply.

He slammed the door and came back. His hands were shaking, his pasty face was now red and his mean, thin lips blue.

'Sorry about that, Inspector. Now where was we? Did you say that somebody was shot dead?'

'I did,' Angel said.

His jaw dropped. 'No. I didn't hear no shots. Where was this?'

'In a car at the entrance to Pleasant's scrapyard.'

His little eyes flashed. 'Didn't hear a thing, Inspector. Honest.'

'Did anything unusual happen round here this afternoon?'

'No. Nothing. I thought the scrapyard didn't open on a Sunday. Who was shot dead then?'

Suddenly there was a scream from somewhere. It was a woman's voice. 'Samson! Samson! Who are you talking to? Do you know there's a puddle of water on the landing? Have you let that dog in again?'

He looked towards the staircase and yelled, 'Well mop it up, for god's sake.'

He turned to Angel, held up his hands and said, 'It's like this all day. That's the wife.'

Angel said, 'I shall want to speak to her. I shall want to speak to everyone in the house. What about guests? How many have you staying with you. Can I see your register?'

The door at the end of the hall slammed. A girl about 14 or 15 wandered through.

'There's nobody else. Just the wife and daughter. Trade is very bad. It's the weekend.' Tickle lifted up the register. 'Have a look but there's nobody in.'

'Nobody at all today? Or yesterday.'

'No.'

The girl shuffled up to the counter, three fingers in her mouth, hair over her face. She stood next to Angel. He smiled at her. She turned up her nose and looked away.

Tickle stared at her with angry eyes.

Angel thought he wanted to say something to her.

Tickle licked his lips and said, 'Marcia, you should be in the back. You know your mother doesn't let you come out here.'

'S'orlright. There's nobody in. I want ten quid, Dad. Give me ten quid and I'll go out.'

Tickle shook his head and looked in pain. He turned to Angel. 'My daughter, Marcia. This is Inspector Angel.'

Angel nodded. 'Did you hear any gunshots, Marcia. Outside here. About an hour ago?'

'Naw,' she said without looking at him.

'Did you see anything happening unusual at the scrap dealer's across the way?'

'Naw.'

She was still gazing at Tickle with her hand held out.

Tickle growled then felt in his pocket, pulled out a small fold of notes, pulled out a ten-pound note, handed it to her and said, 'Now get out of here and don't tell your mother.'

She took it, turned and ran towards the door at the end of the hall.

A voice boomed from the staircase. 'Don't tell your mother, what?'

Angel turned round. A tall, curvaceous, handsome woman in a smart, sleeveless floral dress carrying a bucket and mop, which looked incongruous in her hands, stepped down off the bottom step. He observed that her hair, make-up and nails were all carefully maintained. Angel thought she was a pretty woman who wasn't very happy.

It was Mrs Tickle. She stepped into the hall.

The door banged. Marcia had gone.

Tickle looked his wife straight in the face and said, 'I've given 'er a couple of quid and told 'er off for coming out front.'

She wasn't pleased. She didn't believe him. She turned to Angel and smiled. She had a small, pretty mouth.

Tickle said: 'Joanie, this here is Inspector Angel. The police.'

Joan Tickle's eyes bounced then she smiled quickly. 'Ooo, Inspector Angel,' she said. 'Whatever can we do for you?'

Angel asked her the questions he had asked her husband and her daughter, and she gave the same replies as they had done.

'Oh dear. Who has been shot then?'

He hesitated. 'We're not sure,' he said. 'Well, thank you very much. If you hear of anything or remember anything, please contact me at the police station, will you?'

'Yes, of course,' she said. 'How awful. Just outside here and we never knew about it?'

Angel turned away from the counter and made for the front door.

'Good afternoon, Inspector,' she said charmingly.

'Good afternoon.'

Immediately, in a very different tone, he heard her say, 'You've let that dog in again, Samson Tickle. There's a pool of water on the landing.'

'Why don't you just mop it up?'

'I have done. Where is it now?'

'Oh. It's nothing. I'll take a look,' he growled. 'In its kennel, I expect.'

'Huh! How much money did you give her?'

Angel reached the door and stepped outside. He didn't wait to hear Tickle's next lie. He was glad to be out of the smelly place and into the sunshine. He turned right and made for the terraced house next door.

Angel and Gawber discovered nothing helpful from the house-to-house. Nobody had seen anything unusual or heard any gun shots, which confirmed Angel's thoughts that the murderer had used a gun with a silencer.

They returned to the scrapyard to find that a low loader had arrived, and was lined up ready to winch the Bentley on to the trailer as soon as SOCO had completed its on-site routine of checks.

Angel went inside the marquee. There were four men in whites hovering round the car driver's door. They were just about ready to open it to transfer the body on to a post-mortem stretcher table placed alongside.

DS Taylor came across to Angel and said: 'Funny thing, sir. There are no fingerprints on the door handle. The dead man isn't wearing gloves, yet the door handle has been wiped clean.'

Angel blinked, frowned, turned back to Taylor and said, 'The victim, after stopping, unlocking and opening the yard gates, wouldn't get back in the car, lower the window and wipe the door handle from the inside, would he?'

Taylor shrugged. He couldn't explain it. 'Knew you'd want to know, sir. That's all.'

He nodded. 'That's right, lad.' He frowned.

'Everybody ready?' Dr Mac said.

There were nods and grunts indicating their agreement. Mac grabbed the powerful lamp, put his gloved hand on the car door handle and pulled it open.

The victim's blood-soaked right arm slid off the steering wheel and flopped down. The SOCO photographer stepped forward and took a string of photographs. Then Mac went up very close with the lamp and began to look over every inch of the body and the surround before it was transferred to the stretcher.

Angel didn't need a powerful light and magnifying glass to notice something very unusual, something that was to concern him for some time to come. The smartly dressed dead man in the driving seat had no shoes on.

CHAPTER 3

As Angel considered the strangeness of this revelation, Mac and the others in the white suits began the exacting business of transferring the body to the stretcher. At the same time, in the street outside the marquee, a low-slung, powerful car came to a halt with a loud squeal of brakes. It stopped in front of the blue and white POLICE LINE – DO NOT CROSS tape, and a busty blonde, with legs so long it must have been snowing at the top got out, lifted up the tape and rushed determinedly towards the white marquee.

PC Weightman saw her coming. He rushed in front of her, raised his hands and said, 'No, Miss. No, Miss. You must stay behind the tape. Behind the tape, Miss, if you please.'

Her face was red and her eyes watery and frightened. 'What's happened? I heard that Charles has been shot. Is that right? And that he's dead. Shot dead. I'm Charles Pleasant's … partner. Is that right? Oh no. Say it isn't.'

'Behind the tape, Miss, if you please,' Weightman said, trying to turn her round by her elbows.

She didn't move backwards at all. She wriggled free. 'Tell me. Please. Is Charles Pleasant dead?'

'I'm not sure, Miss. But you must go behind the tape. This is a crime scene and—'

‘But you don’t understand,’ she cried. ‘If he is dead, I know who’s done it. I know exactly who has done it. You must let me through. Besides, I’m his next of kin. I’ve a right to know.’

‘Yes, Miss. But behind the tape, if you please.’

‘I want to see whoever’s in charge?’

PC Donohue licked his lips, rubbed his chin and looked down at the marquee. He took in the situation and came over. They exchanged a few words and Donohue went off to the marquee.

Weightman stayed with the woman. ‘We’ll see what we can do, Miss,’ he said, while shepherding her back under the tape.

Standing outside the marquee was Gawber. Donohue said something to him. Gawber nodded, and went into the marquee.

The young woman wiped her eyes with a tiny tissue.

Weightman sighed and rubbed his chin. He wanted to put his arm round her but he didn’t.

‘Is Mr Pleasant dead, do you know?’

Weightman shook his head. ‘I really don’t know. The body has not been identified as far as I know.’

A few moments later a sombre-faced Angel came out of the marquee, had a few more words with Gawber and then gazed around.

Weightman held up a hand to get his attention.

Angel saw him standing next to the blonde. He walked the few yards up the road, lifted up the tape and went up to them.

‘This is the lady who says she knows who has committed the murder, sir,’ he said.

‘Thanks John,’ he said.

Weightman returned to guarding the tape.

Angel looked wide-eyed at the woman. He noted the tanned tearful face, the long blonde hair and the fruit salad figure. She teetered anxiously up to him. He noticed the excessively high-heeled shoes and guessed they’d come with an excessively high price tag. He also took in the smell of

French perfume. At the right time, it could have been more dangerous than a blackjack.

'You in charge?' she said tearfully.

He nodded. 'DI Angel. You are Charles Pleasant's partner, and you say you know who murdered him?'

'He is dead? I knew it. I knew Emlyn would do it one day. Yes. My name is Jazmin Frazer, my maiden name. It used to be Jones. I've been with Charles for four years now. Oh, whatever am I going to do?'

'Sorry to have to break the sad news to you, Miss Frazer.'

'It was too good to last. It really was.' She began to cry again.

He hesitated, but the question he wanted to ask couldn't wait. 'You said that you know who murdered him.'

She looked up. Her lips tightened. 'Oh yes. Yes. Indeed I do.' She sniffed. 'My ex-husband. Well, he's no man, more of a snake. Emlyn Jones, the antiques dealer. That's who's murdered my Charles.'

Angel's eyebrows shot up. He knew Jones. An oily, creepy sort of a man. Served two years for drunken driving. Hit a phone box. Was found unconscious with a half-dressed underage girl drunk out of her skull projected through the windscreen from the seat beside him. Indeed Angel had interviewed him several times over the years. His name was frequently cropping up, but he had never been able to make anything stick.

'Why would he want to do that?'

'Jealousy. Jealous as hell he was. When I told him I was leaving him, he just laughed. He couldn't believe that anybody would take a fancy to me. He went wild when he heard it was Charles. He threw two pieces of Rockingham into the fireplace – smashed into a thousand pieces. Twelve hundred pounds just like that.'

'Has a son, hasn't he?'

She sniffed. 'He's my son, too. Yes. Stanley.'

Angel knew Stanley too. He was no saint.

He licked his lips. 'How did Emlyn Jones come to know Charles Pleasant then?'

'Knew him from way back. They're about the same age. Went to school together.' Tears welled up again. 'Oh dear, what am I going to do?'

Angel pursed his lips. He wasn't much good at comforting witnesses, especially glamorous ones. Weeping women made him as soft as a Strangeways dumpling, and were such an embarrassment.

'Do you know why your husband turned up here on a Sunday? I mean, was there really any business to be done on a hot, Sunday August afternoon?'

'Said it was an appointment. Somebody rang this morning. He was meeting somebody with … something. I don't know what exactly. Half past four. Couldn't come tomorrow, I think he said. Charles wouldn't miss a deal if there was profit in it.'

Angel frowned. An appointment? It was both interesting and dreadful: an appointment to be murdered. Nobody was hanging around with any scrap to sell.

'Didn't give a name, I suppose?'

'Didn't say.'

He shook his head. He couldn't stay any longer with her. He would have to go back to the scene. Moving the body might reveal more evidence. This wasn't a good time. There was too much to do.

'Do you live in town?'

'Creesforth Road. The Hacienda.'

He remembered it. He had passed it several times. Reminded him of a Mexican ranch he'd seen on American westerns. White stucco front. Outside porch, upstairs balcony. Fountain out front. Incongruous among the other expensive houses on that road.

He nodded. He pulled out his mobile phone and muttered something into it. Then he turned back. 'I am sending a WPC back with you, Miss Frazer, and I'll be in touch tomorrow. Thank you for your assistance and please accept my sincere condolences.'

She seemed more controlled then, and was clearly comforted by his few words.

'You're very kind,' she said and turned away.

He called Weightman over, whispered something, then lifted the tape and ducked under it.

Gawber came rushing up.

Angel wrinkled his nose. 'She says her ex-husband did it.'

Gawber frowned, then shook his head. 'Can't imagine anyone deliberately removing their shoes and socks to murder somebody outside, sir.'

'I know her from somewhere. Says her maiden name is Jazmin Frazer. Ring any bells, Ron?'

'No, sir. Can't say it does.'

'Wasn't it her sister, Bridie Longley, used to be Frazer, that was found in pieces in an oil drum on the A1 in Leicestershire?'

Angel stopped the BMW on a narrow road in the older part of Bromersley town. He parked on double yellow lines. Being Sunday, almost all the town centre shops were closed; the streets were quiet, resulting in plenty of room to park. He got out of the car right outside The Old Curiosity Shop. It was a big shop with many tiny windows in the frontage and the door. The windows were not decorated in themselves, but the shop stock was clearly to be seen through them. Through any pane of glass could be seen a jumble of antiques plus toys of yesteryear, such as a penny-farthing bicycle, a large Victorian doll's house and a ventriloquist's doll in a proportionately small dinner jacket.

Outside and high up on the outside wall was a white alarm box with the words 'Potts Security' stencilled on it in blue. Above that were three windows along the length of the wall with strips of pretty floral curtains visible at the sides.

He went up to the door. It had a neat sign in the window advising that the shop was closed. Nevertheless, he found the bell push and leaned on it for a couple of minutes. There was no response. It surely would have roused Rip Van Winkle.

He repeated the action and received curious looks from a young couple passing by.

Suddenly he saw a smiling man with shining eyes and a short beard appear inside the shop. It was Emlyn Jones. He was looking especially smart, wearing a dinner jacket. When he saw that Angel had seen him, he rushed to unlock the door.

'Oh, so very pleased to see you, Inspector Angel,' he said in a breathy, Welsh voice. 'Please come in. So very nice of you to call.'

He was almost always smiling.

Angel nodded and went into the shop. He had been there several times over the years, so the style of the man in no way surprised him. He always looked smart, but that evening he looked smarter than usual.

Jones shot a bolt across the door behind him and locked it.

'Come this way, Inspector. You want to see me about something important? You must do, calling at this time on a Sunday evening. Look, bless you, it is half past six. Please come this way. You will be missing evensong, I know. It's a sacrifice we have to make when we are in business or in a profession, like you and me. When I was at home in Swansea, I would never have missed chapel, Inspector. It wouldn't have been allowed. It was a tradition and a discipline to keep us on the track of honesty, integrity and, and, to remind us of those *beautiful* Ten Commandments.'

He led the way past a life-sized teddy bear, an upright piano with two brass candleholders across the front of it and a box of fisherman's glass floats, a big doll with a pincushion for a stomach with all kinds of old-fashioned hat pins, some twelve inches long, with pearl, brightly coloured glass or Whitby jet ends sticking out of it. On the shelves were various glass vases, goldfish bowls, chamber pots filled with water and each with a red rubber ball floating on the top. Angel frowned and wondered if the floating balls were there to check the wholeness of the pot. Jones took him to a small door with a brass knob. It led into a cubbyhole under the stairs, which had been turned into the tiniest of offices. It had little more in it than a desk, a small cupboard and three chairs.

'Find a seat you like, Inspector Angel. I will join you directly. Would you like to join me in a glass of port?'

'No thank you,' he said sitting on a plush antique chair.

He looked round the tidy little office and was surprised to see four large parsnip roots piled together on top of the low cupboard. He lowered his eyebrows as he considered how they came to be there. There didn't seem to be any cooking facilities in sight. He remembered Jones had a delightful kitchen in the flat above the shop.

Jones suddenly saw the parsnips and reacted strangely. He was clearly embarrassed. His eyes flashed and he initially put his hands over the parsnips to hide them. Then he looked at Angel and smiled, then he opened the cupboard door, snatched them up and stuffed them quickly on a shelf in there and then clattered some glasses together. He came out with a glass and bottle and with a big smile on his face, showed it to Angel. 'The very best,' he said and brandished the label.

'Not just now,' Angel repeated.

'Very well,' he said still smiling. He placed the glass on the desk, poured the wine into it, put the cork in the bottle, returned the bottle to the cupboard and sat down opposite Angel. 'Now,' he said. 'Are you comfortable. It is so long since I have seen you. This is nice. Now, what can I do you for you, Inspector?'

Angel sighed. He began slowly. 'I met your ex-wife, Jazmin, this afternoon. Never met her before.'

Jones' face changed briefly. The leering smile left him. He took a deep breath. The smile returned. 'What did the cow want,' he said, still beaming.

'She told me that you murdered Charles Pleasant,' he said evenly.

The smile went again. His hands went in the air. His eyes stared and his face changed to that of a man in agony.

'So my friend Charles is dead? Oh, how dreadful. How awful. It is a sin. A great sin. I went to school with him, you know. We are the same age. Oh dear. Well, well. Oh, I will sing a Psalm to his memory tonight, Inspector. Two Psalms. Oh, how I wish I could have had gone to chapel this evening. But how perfectly shameful of you, Inspector … to believe that I might have had anything to do with it. I am surprised that you took any notice of that bitch. She would say anything to besmirch my good name.'

Angel stifled a smile. He was not aware that Jones had a good name.

Jones then looked at the glass of port, wrinkled his nose and pushed it away.

'What happened? When did this tragedy happen?'

'He was shot. This afternoon at about twenty minutes past four,' Angel said: 'Where were you at twenty minutes past four?'

The smile returned.

'I was with my son – you know my son, Stanley – at the celebratory luncheon at The Feathers, to mark the opening of Potts's new offices,' he replied. 'I was surprised that Charles had not been there. If he had been a client of Potts, he would have had an invitation. Of course, if he had another appointment, if he was money grubbing on the Sabbath … tut tut. If he had been there, maybe his death could have been … avoided.'

'Is there anybody who can actually confirm that you and your son were actually at The Feathers at twenty past four?'

His eyes twinkled and he raised his eyebrows and kept them raised. 'Oh yes, Inspector. I think so,' he said, smiling and rocking his head confidently from side to side.

Angel didn't see it coming. 'Who?' he said.

'There was your Superintendent Harker for one.'

Angel blinked.

'I think you know him?' he said with a grin. 'And then there were about a hundred and twenty other guests.'

Angel nodded. He saw that he had walked into a set up. He recovered quickly. 'Can you think of anyone who would have benefited from Charles Pleasant's death?' he said, then added deviously, 'Apart from yourself.'

'Oh Inspector Angel, you have a mischievous mind. It must be all those criminals you are mixing with. Their wickedness is rubbing off on to you. You compel me to say that I have absolutely nothing to gain from the death of poor, dear, Charles. Nothing at all.'

'Maybe it was to get back at your ex-wife taking up with him?'

The smile vanished. 'She was crossed off four years ago, Inspector. February, 2003. The whore departed,' he declared and the smile returned. 'That Easter, never did I sing *The Easter Hymn* by Mascagni better.'

Angel sighed. He rubbed his chin. 'What about your son? Where is he now?'

'Ah. You have me there, dear Inspector. We left the reception together at The Feathers at around five o'clock. He brought me here and then I think he may have returned to his flat. These young people … there's no telling where they are or what they're up to. Probably now out with a young lady; or in his flat, teaching her to play the harp.'

'He doesn't live here anymore?'

'He's had his own flat for four years now, Inspector. When I threw that bitch out—'

'I thought she divorced you?'

'The divorce was … mutual,' he said. 'Expensive, but mutual, dear Inspector. When I threw that bitch out, I thought it healthier for Stanley to have a place of his own. She is his mother, after all. I can't change that, although I wish that I could. I let him create his own establishment so that she could visit him without me tripping up over her and falling into any more of her feminine trickery. Women can be so deceitful, don't you think, Inspector? They can think up evil and sinfulness so much more easily than straightforward feeble men like us. You must have come across that in your long experience of studying crime, Inspector?'

Angel shook his head. 'So what's his address?' he said.

'I am sure he would love to see you, but I don't think he will be at home, right now. You could telephone him.'

'I may call on him tomorrow.'

'Tomorrow would be good. He will be here all day. You would be sure to catch him.'

'His address and phone number, please.'

'Of course. It is Flat 14, Council Close, Potts New Estate. Telephone 223942.'

It was half past eight before Angel reached home that night. Mary wasn't pleased. He hadn't managed to eat anything since the lunch they had had together at about twelve, noon.

'You'll put yourself on your back if you don't eat regular meals,' she said. 'That's what gave your father that ulcer.'

'Yes, well, there wasn't anywhere … open. It's Sunday.'

'You must eat proper meals at regular intervals.'

The roast beef sirloin joint Mary had planned for serving at around 6 p.m. had been left to cool on the work top and covered with a wire-framed linen protector.

'Would you like a slice of cold beef, Yorkshire pudding and gravy? That's the best suggestion I can make.'

He nodded thankfully, opened a tin of German beer out of the fridge and settled down at the kitchen table.

'You know what it's like,' he said. 'It's strike while the iron's hot. I like to be where it's happening. There's always some little thing that the system doesn't necessarily include that might point to the murderer.'

'Hmmm,' she said sceptically as she poured batter across the bottom of the blisteringly hot pan. 'And has it worked for you this time?'

He pulled a face. 'No. Although I might have missed a footprint.'

'Your scenes of crimes team would have picked that up, wouldn't they?'

'Probably. But this was a very unusual footprint. I simply needed to be there.'

Mary closed the oven door. 'Oh,' she said, sitting at the table with him.

He sipped the beer. It tasted good.

'It was a footprint of the murderer,' he added. 'When he shot the victim, he was in his bare feet.'

'Bare feet? Why would the murderer walk about in bare feet? Are you sure it was human?'

'Yes, of course.'

'Why did he take his shoes off then? Was it so that he could creep up behind the victim or something?'

'I don't know why. He had no need to. He was in the street ... about twenty feet away from the man when he shot him.'

'Where did he keep his shoes then? In his pockets? You don't know if he was dressed or not, do you?'

'No, but I suppose he had trousers on, at least. He wouldn't get far in Bromersley without them, would he? It was a summer's day. Sebastopol Terrace was quiet, but he had to get away. It was a cul-de-sac. He would have to get away somehow, either on foot or in a car.'

'He couldn't drive a car in bare feet, could he?'

He licked his lips and frowned. 'Now, there's a thing.'

'Are you sure the foot marks belonged to the murderer?'

'The angle of entry of the bullets into the victim fits, the range fits, there were discarded shell cases on the floor in front of the footprints. Everything says the murderer had no shoes and socks on, but why?'

Mary frowned.

'There's something else,' he said. 'The murdered man was shot in a car and he also had no shoes on. He had socks on, but no shoes. He was smartly dressed. Reid and Taylor worsted, handmade bespoke suit, gold cufflinks, white shirt and tie, but no shoes.'

'It would be hard to drive in his stocking feet.'

'Very difficult. Uncomfortable, pressing on the pedals, especially the brake. What would be the point?' He ran his hand through his hair. 'It's going to beat me, Mary, this is. It's crazy.'

'No it won't. You'll solve it,' she said confidently. She stood up and moved to the sink. 'You always have done,' she added.

He shook his head. She'd more faith in him than he had in himself.

'Wasn't there a shoe fetish murderer Wakefield way a few years ago?' she said.

'Mmmm. It was a very strange case. He raped women then murdered them, then stole their shoes.'

'Maybe this murderer misses out on the rape, commits the murder and steals the shoes?'

'Both the murderer and the victim are without shoes. One has socks on, one hasn't. Doesn't make sense.'

Mary was standing in front of the oven stirring a small pan of gravy. She suddenly shuddered. 'It's awful. And dangerous. That's what you've been doing this afternoon, is it? Looking for a murdering lunatic who murders people in his bare feet. Why don't you get a proper job? Like a teacher or something? At least it's decent and … honourable and safe, dealing with children all day.'

Angel wrinkled his nose. 'We've been through this, Mary, many a time. You know it's a necessary service … to the community. Somebody needs to do it.'

'Yes, but why you?' she snapped. 'It's dirty. It's dealing with all sorts of unsavoury people. And it's downright dangerous!'

He was caught, unable to find a reply.

'The truth is you enjoy it!' she added triumphantly.

He couldn't deny it. He sighed. He unfolded his serviette and then fiddled with his knife and fork.

'Oh!' she whooped. 'Yorkshire pudding's almost ready. Carve what you want. I'm past it, now. Couldn't eat a thing.'

CHAPTER 4

'Good morning, sir. You wanted me?'

'Yes. Good morning, Ron. Come in. Sit down.'

Gawber closed the office door.

Angel told Gawber about his interview the previous evening with Emlyn Jones.

'I remember him, sir. Oily individual. Could talk for Wales. With a sickly smile that never went away.'

'It went away when we talked about his ex-wife,' Angel said.

They exchanged knowing glances.

'I didn't get to see their son, Stanley. No reply when I phoned him. No doubt tipped off by his father. I left it until today; however, it'll have to be done later. Maybe this evening. I don't want to interview him with his father around.'

'Do you want me to?'

'No. I'll catch up with him. There's plenty I want you to see to. Emlyn Jones. See if you can find anything on his ex-wife, Jazmin Jones aka Jazmin Frazer, also her late sister, Bridie Longley aka Bridie Frazer, on the PNC.'

The phone rang.

'Right, sir,' Gawber said and went out.

Angel nodded and picked up the phone.

It was DS Taylor. 'We're still here, going through Pleasant's yard and office, sir. There's a man turned up for work. Says his name is Molloy. I thought you might want to speak to him.'

'Yes, of course. Keep him there. I'll come straightaway.'

The small yard was a tight jumble of crashed cars, refrigerators, oil drums, washing machines and unidentifiable lumps of metal in all shapes, colours and sizes. It was in piles stacked as high as fifteen feet in places. In between the piles was a track, wide enough to enable a vehicle to be driven through the junk to the one-storey breeze block building at the back.

In the doorway of the building stood a middle-aged man with his hands in his pockets. He was watching the SOCOs in their white forensic overalls around the yard, picking up pieces of scrap, looking at them, dropping them down behind them and moving on. Occasionally the man looked down at his trainers and kicked the dust like a frisky young pony.

Angel drove the BMW round the circle and stopped behind the SOCO van. He got out of the car and walked up to him. He introduced himself and found out that the man was called Grant Molloy.

'You the manager, here?' Angel said.

'I was the manager. Well, I was the only one here. I ran the business for Mr Pleasant … single-handed. He was hardly ever here. In fact, I can't think what he was doing here yesterday, a beautiful sunny Sunday afternoon like it was. Hottest day for years. Can't think that anybody'd be bringing scrap in at that time. Besides, he scarcely knew copper from 24-carat gold. Anyway, who would want to do a terrible thing like this? It's like the Wild West.'

'Have you any idea who would profit from Mr Pleasant's death?'

'No. Nobody.'

'Nobody at all?' Angel said. 'Difficult traders who felt they hadn't had a fair deal?'

'It would be me they would take their revenge out on. I was on the front line.'

Angel nodded thoughtfully.

'It don't look as if I'm going to get another wage packet out of this place,' Molloy said. 'Does it?'

'I don't know who Mr Pleasant will have left the business to, but there is bound to be somebody, and presumably they would like you to stay. Do you know Miss Jazmin Frazer? She's the most likely one to know, I should think.'

'I've met her,' he said. 'I suppose I should go round and see her.'

'It might be a good idea.'

Molloy nodded then said: 'Aye, maybe I will, but I won't stay here, Mr Angel. It's time I moved on. This wasn't a proper business, you know. There could be weeks pass, and I'd only take in a few hundredweight of mixed scrap mostly from regular totters and scroungers. You will know that since scrap dealers had to be registered, it became too big a risk to be accepting sheets of lead and the like, and that used to be the cream of the business. The boss was quite definite about not accepting scrap from doubtful sources. I think he once said he only kept the business going because his grandfather started it and he hadn't the heart to shut it down. It was a tax loss. That's what it was, he said, a tax loss.'

Angel rubbed his chin.

He asked him further questions about the running of the business, and Molloy took him into the office, unlocked the small, built-in safe in which there was a receipt book, an accounts book and £600 in mixed notes. The arrangement was that Mr Pleasant regularly provided Molloy with a float of a £1,000 and Molloy had that week paid out £400, to totters and people who had brought scrap in. The list of the amounts was in the accounts book and the names and addresses on the carbon copy of the receipt with the cash paid out and description of the scrap received and the weight. Pleasant called in, usually on Monday morning, checked the cash and made the float back up to £1,000.

Angel took possession of Molloy's keys, gave him an informal receipt and was taking note of his address.

There was a noise behind him. It was Taylor.

'Excuse me, sir. Could you get the gentleman to move the forklift? There's stuff behind we need to take a look at.'

Molloy said: 'It don't move. Been broken down years. Mr Pleasant had the only key. But I would have thought you could've gotten behind it.'

Taylor said: 'Will you have a look, sir?'

Angel and Molloy followed Taylor out of the office to a yellow, rusty forklift truck that had seen better days. It was backed up close to the side of the office wall, but there were piles of assorted sheets of metal wedged behind it.

Taylor stood there and pointed to the stuff trapped between the perimeter wall of the yard and the back of the forklift.

Angel pursed his lips. It didn't seem that anything could be concealed behind it. It was possible to see pretty well all there was there. He climbed up on to the platform of the forklift and peered down behind it. There were just offcuts from steel sheets. There was no way anything could be concealed. He nodded appropriately and stepped down.

'Shall we leave it, sir?' Taylor said.

Angel looked at the rear of the forklift. 'We can't push it, Don.'

'You'd never move that by hand,' Molloy agreed.

Angel walked round to the front of the forklift and looked down at the parched ground in the sunshine. Something caught his attention. He squatted down and peered closely at the dried earth and the vehicle's front tyres. He stood up and said: 'This has been moved … and not long since. It would be shortly after the last heavy downfall of rain.'

'It couldn't have been,' Molloy said. 'The battery's not been on a charge for two years at least.'

Angel glanced at him, then went to the back of the forklift, unbuckled the plastic cover from over the top of the battery which was under the driver's seat, then looked around for something. It was a matter of finding something convenient that would conduct electricity. He saw two strips of steel plate offcuts, each more than yard long. They were hardly a convenient size, but he touched each battery terminal with the corners of the offcuts and then brought the two steel pieces in close proximity to each other. There was a spark sufficient to show that the battery was lively.

Molloy's jaw dropped open.

Angel discarded the offcuts. 'All we need is the ignition key.' He turned to Taylor. 'Have you got Pleasant's keys?'

Taylor blinked and dug into his pocket and pulled out a small bunch. 'Yes, sir. They were in the gate padlock. We used them to lock up last night.'

Angel nodded.

Taylor jumped on the forklift and began to try to see if he had the key to fit the ignition. He found it. In seconds, he was able to drive it forward the ten feet or so to enable them to work behind it. He pulled on the brake and stepped down from the driving seat.

Angel wasn't interested in what was behind it. He had already looked at that from the platform of the truck. His interest was in what might be underneath it. And he was not disappointed. There was a thin steel sheet about four feet long by two feet wide set on top of well-trodden earth. He stepped forward, lifted it up and pushed it to one side.

Molloy and Taylor looked on, surprised at Angel's unexpected move.

Underneath the steel plate, in an excavated hole, on its back, was a large old iron safe. He nodded with satisfaction and stepped forward to look closely at the door. He recognized the make. It was a Philips Mark II made in Birmingham in the 1930s. He had some idea what the key would look like. He looked at Taylor. 'You've got the keys, Don. Is there one on the bunch to fit this?'

Taylor reached up to the ignition of the forklift, took out the keys, glanced at them, looked at Angel who with a gesture invited him to toss them down to him. He caught them easily and quickly went through them and instantly knew it wasn't there. He tossed them back and rubbed his chin. He peered down at the safe and found a serial number stamped neatly on a small brass-coloured plate under the handle. '12574'. He wrote it down on the back of an envelope.

'There's nothing more we can do about that until we get the key.' He reached down, picked up the steel sheet and threw it back across the top of the safe. Then he instructed Taylor to reverse the fork lift and leave it as it was.

Molloy had been standing silently when Angel discovered that the battery was charged and the forklift was in working order and that there was a safe hidden underneath it. When Angel questioned him, he said he knew nothing at all about it and thereafter he left his home address and took his leave.

Angel rubbed his chin. He took out his mobile and tapped in a number. It was soon answered. It was PC Ahaz.

'Ahmed, I want you to look up the telephone number of Philips Safes in Birmingham in the address book on my table. You'll need to ask to speak to a specified name and then give them a specific code word – both are in my book – before they will tell you anything helpful. It's their security routine, all right? When you've gone through that, ask them if they would be good enough to send by registered post a key for one of their safes. It is a Mark II and the serial number is 12574. All right?'

'Got that, sir.'

'Also, I want you to ask Inspector Asquith if he would be good enough to organize a full-time security watch on these premises from 1700 hours today until 0830 hours tomorrow.'

He closed the mobile, pushed it into his pocket. He looked round for Taylor who was with other SOCOs, turning over the scrap metal. He went up to him and said, 'By the way, Ron, I want you to lift the street grates.'

'I thought you would, sir. We'll do that on the way out. How far do you want us to go?'

'Just to the end of this street. Being a cul-de-sac, it's the only way the murderer could have gone. If he was on foot, he wouldn't want to have carried the gun far.'

'Right, sir.'

'And see if there are any shoes on your travels.'

'Shoes. Right, sir.'

Angel then said: 'By the way, the plaster cast of that footprint, I hope you've got it somewhere safe?'

'It's on my desk at the station, sir.'

'Good. When you've finished here, I want you to make forty-three copies of it. I want to send each force a plaster cast.'

Taylor raised his eyebrows. 'Great idea. Then at each force CID, when a likely candidate comes into their hands, they'll be able to check on the spot whether he's our man or not. A bit of a twist on the prince fitting the slipper on Cinderella, sir?'

Angel nodded grimly, then shrugged. 'I've nothing else to go on.'

He pointed the bonnet of the BMW along Creesforth Road and through the open gates of the big white detached house, The Hacienda. He steered round the marble fountain, pulled up in front of the white steps, got out, glanced at the spray of water shooting out of the mouth of the angelic marble figure facing the blue sky, then ran up the steps on to a balcony. He stepped forward to the giant wooden arched door, found the iron handle at the side of it and pulled it down several times. He heard bells ring from somewhere distant. He waited for what seemed a long time and there was no response. He was beginning to think that Jazmin Frazer was out when he heard a woman's voice call out above the sound of the fountain spray: 'Inspector!'

He looked round.

'Inspector Angel, I am here.'

He saw her to his left. It was Jazmin Frazer in a white towelling robe. She had come up the side of the house from the back and was standing at the corner by a building that appeared to be garages.

She waved him to join her.

'Will you come this way?'

He responded with a hand, turned, walked down the steps, along the front of the house to the corner and joined her.

'How nice to see you. I am outside, by the pool. Do you enjoy the sun?'

'Yes, I suppose I do,' he said and followed the long legs down the side of the house to the rear of the building which opened out into a huge swimming pool and a long view of the Pennines behind.

The sun was shining and there wasn't a cloud in the sky.

She pointed to an upright canvas chair and a sunbed with a headrest. 'Take your pick,' she said.

Although the sunbed looked inviting, he chose the upright chair. He wouldn't have looked the part in his regular working suit.

'Can I get you a drink or anything?' she said. 'Name your poison. A cool beer?'

He was tempted, but he said, 'No thank you. I won't keep you above a couple of minutes.'

'No rush, Inspector. I am really pleased to see you. It has been very quiet here since … since yesterday.'

Angel nodded sympathetically.

She went up to the full length sun bed, threw off the white robe to reveal that she was wearing a white bikini which really showed how brown she was. She lowered herself on to it and stretched out comfortably as if she intended remaining there the entire day.

'Did you arrest Emlyn, then?'

'No. Emlyn Jones said that he and your son were at a reception at The Feathers at the critical time of 4.20 yesterday afternoon.'

Her head shot round. 'He's lying.'

'I will check it out thoroughly, but he said that my boss, Superintendent Harker, was also there.'

'You'll find he's lying.'

'And about another hundred and twenty guests?'

'They're lying. Must be. I tell you. I know him. I worshipped Emlyn Jones. I used to believe every word he said. I thought he was so … so honest. I can't understand it … the lying, hypocritical, Welsh bastard.'

Angel shook his head. 'I'll check on it, most carefully, rest assured.'

'If you have eyewitnesses, Inspector, then he paid them to lie. He's like that. You can't trust him an inch.'

He shook his head. 'I've got to do things by the book, Miss Frazer. But have no fear, I shall check out every word he utters … as I do with everybody's evidence,' he added.

'I should hope so. And when you have done that, you'll find that I'm right.'

He wanted to move on. It wasn't easy, as she was quite worked up about her ex-husband.

'Mr Pleasant,' Angel said. 'Did he have an arrangement to see somebody at the scrapyard yesterday?'

'I believe so. Yes.'

'Did he tell you who it was?'

'I think he simply said it was business. I took that to mean that it wasn't worth mentioning who it was or what it was about. It was somebody I wouldn't have heard of. It was, I assumed, somebody simply bringing something to sell him. Scrap metal. That's all I know.'

'When was the arrangement made?'

'I really don't know. We were out by the pool. We had had a light lunch. At about three, he had a swim. Then dried off on the lounger, went in the house, came out a few minutes later in his suit … said he was nipping down to the yard and wouldn't be long.'

'Did you know that when he was found, he was not wearing shoes?'

She turned, whipped off the sunglasses and said, 'Not wearing shoes?'

'That's right.'

'That's … ridiculous. I am sure he left here wearing shoes. He wouldn't be able to get around … to the garage here to get the car out.'

'Nevertheless, that's how he was found. In his stockinged feet.'

'I wouldn't let him turn out of the house without shoes. It's ridiculous. What happened to them? Why would he take off his shoes? He wouldn't have been seen outside the house without shoes … only on a beach … on the deck of a yacht … in a swimming pool … in the bedroom. Did he still have his socks on?'

'Yes. He was fully dressed apart from his shoes and we still haven't found them. I need a description, if you please.'

'Well, really,' she said petulantly. There was a pause. 'Black polished leather. Plain fronts. Elasticated sides. Size nine.'

He took an envelope out of his inside pocket and wrote it down. 'Thank you. Was there anything special about them?'

'Special? No. He bought them in town. He would only wear leather for regular, business occasions. They were polished and shining. Fussy about his appearance, Charles was,' she muttered thoughtfully. 'I don't understand why he would be without shoes.'

'You were not actually married to Mr Pleasant, were you, Miss Frazer?'

'No.'

He pursed his lips, gave a little shrug and said, 'I have to ask this, Miss Frazer. It may seem indelicate at this time, but it has to be asked. Who benefits from the death of Mr Pleasant?'

'I do, of course. He left everything to me. I am not the least bit embarrassed by it, Inspector. It's the way of the world. And I don't mind telling you that I would give it all up to have Charles walk through that door and know that he was alive and well.'

'I know. I am only sorry it can't be done.'

She nodded.

'Forgive me, if I continue,' he said gently. 'There's a safe at the scrapyard, Miss Frazer. I wondered if you knew anything about it. In particular if you had a key for it … here … or anywhere?'

'No. There'd be a key on Charles's key ring, I think. Molloy has a key for it, I believe. I'm pretty sure Charles had said that he had. He has to have access to cash to pay out.'

'That's the safe in the office. I meant another safe. A much bigger one.'

Jazmin Frazer blinked. 'I don't know anything much about the business, Inspector.'

A mobile phone began to ring.

'Excuse me,' he said. He stood up and plunged his hand into his pocket.

It was Ahmed.

'Sorry to bother you, sir. Two things.'

'Yes?'

'The super wants to see you urgently.'

'Didn't say what for?'

'No, sir.'

'Right. And the other?'

'I phoned Philips and went through the routine as you instructed, sir, but they said that the records of all their safes manufactured before 1939 were destroyed when their factory was blown up by a bomb in the blitz in 1942.'

Angel wrinkled his nose. That was a disappointment. 'Right, lad. Ta. Tell the super I'm on my way.'

He frowned and slowly closed the phone. He thought he had finished all the pressing business he had with Jazmin Frazer.

'I am wanted back at the station,' he said. 'If you will excuse me?'

'Of course.'

He got up to leave.

'Please find poor Charles's shoes,' she said. 'I can't imagine what Emlyn Jones would want with them.'

CHAPTER 5

It was 9.29 hours on Monday, 6 August. A man in overalls and hat appeared from down a ginnel through leafy lanes of accountants', solicitors' and moneylenders' offices on to Huddersfield Road, Bromersley. He was carrying a tiny collapsible metal and canvas stool, a weatherproof canopy and a tool case; he had a small vacuum flask sticking out of a long hip pocket. He sat down on the stool in front of a green telephone connection box set in front of the front wall of a solicitor's office. He put the canopy over the connection box, opened the tool box, took out a screwdriver and began to remove the connection box cover.

Twenty yards away, a small queue of customers began to form outside the Bromersley branch of The Great Northern Bank. There were four young men and then a youngish woman who sported the most enormous bosom and stomach so that she appeared to be close to giving birth to Sheffield Wednesday. Behind her in the queue two other men had arrived.

The bank door was opened with a flourish at 9.30 by a man in a black uniform with silver buttons down the front.

The queue shuffled inside the bank, but as the young woman approached a till, her breathing became uneven and her face contorted as if in great pain; she held her stomach, then collapsed in a heap on the floor.

A few customers turned to assist her. There wasn't much they could do. Her forehead was moist and she was saying, 'I need to go to the bathroom. I need to go to the bathroom.'

The security guard, Cyril Widdowson, the man with the buttons, came up. 'Now Miss, whatever's the matter?'

She gasped. 'I need to use your … bathroom, very, very quickly. Very quickly indeed.'

A woman rushed up and said, 'If you're not careful, she'll have it in here! You should call for an ambulance.'

Widdowson's face went white. 'Right,' he said helping the lumpy woman to her feet. He called to a girl on one of the tills, 'Dial 999 and get an ambulance! Then tell Mr Hobson.'

The lady teller quickly took in the situation. 'Right, Cyril,' she replied.

He put his arm boldly round the big woman and assisted her up to the door leading to the bank vaults, stationery store, back door and lavatory. Then he looked around nervously. He still had certain security procedures to observe. However, there was nothing he could recall in standing orders about collapsing, pregnant women. He peered through a tiny window in the security door. Everything inside seemed normal. There was nobody near them on this side. He checked that the CCTV camera had them in its range. The situation seemed secure. He tapped the day's code into the lock and the door clicked open.

'Where's the bathroom,' she wailed as they went through the door into the secure area. The security door closed behind them.

Widdowson directed her to the lavatory door. 'Will you be all right?'

She staggered through the door without replying and quickly slammed it shut. She shot the bolt across with a bang.

He stood outside, sighed and tried not to be alarmed as he heard groans and moans. He dreaded to think what the result of all the noises might be.

There was the sound of a buzzer. It was the noise caused by somebody wanting to get into the secure area.

He crossed over to the security door and looked through the tiny window. It was the bank manager, Mr Hobson.

Widdowson rushed to open the door to admit him.

Hobson came blustering through. He was not a happy man. 'What's happening?'

'A pregnant women, sir. She's in the staff toilet, Mr Hobson. Sounds like she's having it now. Miss Phipps has phoned for an ambulance.'

'Yes. I know. Well, be very careful. We must not lower our security, you know.'

'I couldn't very well deny her use of the lavatory, sir.'

'No. No. I see that. But, well, we'll have to escort her back out of here. Before anything.... Just as soon as we can.'

'Yes, sir.'

Hobson banged on the staff toilet door. 'Are you all right, Miss?'

'Yes,' a quiet little voice said.

Hobson said: 'I'll go out and see if there's any sign of that ambulance.'

He crossed over to the security door, peered through the tiny window at the customers queuing at the tills, and beyond them to the front door. He was just in time to see two men with beards in bright blue and green uniforms rush into the bank hall. The one with 'Paramedic' printed in white across his chest and back was carrying a shoulder bag. The other was carrying a stretcher. They rushed up to a teller's window.

Hobson dashed back to the staff toilet door. 'The ambulance is here now, Miss!'

'I'm coming out now,' she said.

They heard the bolt on the door slide back, the door slowly opened and there she was. Leaning back against the wall, her face perspiring. 'I think my waters have broken.'

Hobson's eyes flashed. 'Can you manage to walk a few steps?' he said.

'I think so.'

Hobson and Widdowson escorted the woman out of the secure area back into the bank hall.

The men sighed with relief when they heard the click of the security door behind them.

'This is the young lady,' he said to the man holding the stretcher. 'She's, er, not very well.'

'I'm a paramedic. We'll soon have you in hospital, love. There's nothing to worry about.'

'Not to worry,' the other man said as he opened the stretcher. 'There we are. Have you there in a jiffy.'

She nodded and tried to smile.

Two minutes later the woman and the two uniformed men were on their way in the ambulance; Mr Hobson was back in his office wiping his forehead with a handkerchief; Cyril Widdowson was in his little cubicle next to the bank vault franking letters ready to take to the post office in his lunch hour, and the man outside, sitting on the stool in front of the solicitor's office next to the bank, smiled, poured himself another cup of coffee from the flask and rested the headphones momentarily round his neck.

The Bromersley branch of The Great Northern Bank resumed its normal business of accepting other people's money, investing other people's money, paying out other people's money and retaining a small but healthy percentage for its directors, staff and shareholders, in the process.

However, after a quiet few minutes had passed, there erupted the most abominable stink from the smallest room, accompanied by a stream of water gushing out under the door.

The smell pervaded Cyril's Widdowson's cubicle, also the sound of running water. He acted immediately. He rushed over to the source of the ghastly smell. He held his nose and pushed open the loo door. Water was running down the wall from the lavatory cistern. He closed the door quickly.

He splashed back to his cubicle, picked up the phone on the wall, pressed a button and the manager, Mr Hobson, answered.

'What is it now, Widdowson?' he said irritably.

'We need a plumber urgently, sir. There's liquid running from the staff toilet and there's the most awful smell.'

'What?' he said. 'Well, get the usual ones. The ones we always use. The ones head office has approved.'

'Right, sir.'

Minutes later, two men with beards in overalls and carrying toolboxes arrived in the bank at the security door and pressed the button.

Widdowson saw them through the window in the security door and opened it two inches.

'What's the trouble?' the older of the two said.

Widdowson peered at them through the crack. 'You're not our usual plumber.'

'No. He can't come himself, he's on an emergency job in Mexborough. We work for him. He said it would be all right if we explained. He said that the caller said it was very urgent. The boss can call later this afternoon when he's finished there. We've come off a job at the Town Hall. Of course, if you don't want us to see to it, we can leave and go back to the job we're on.'

They turned to leave.

The smell from behind and the sound of running water was in Widdowson's ears. His stomach turned over and then turned back again. He opened the door wider and called them back.

'No. I er—'

He swallowed. 'I'll have to check with the manager.'

'Yes, all right, but what exactly is the problem?' the older man said pressing on the door. 'Hadn't you better let us see what it is, while we're here. It might be getting worse. Oh, what a stink!'

The smell was truly awful.

Widdowson hesitated. His grip on the door relaxed a little.

The two men in boiler suits pushed and they were through it, taking the bank guard with them. The door closed and the lock clicked.

'You can't come in here without—'

The leader pulled out a Walther PPK/S and jabbed it in his belly.

Widdowson gasped.

'Turn round, face the wall and shut up,' the leader said.

They bolted the door, pulled on rubber gloves and slid ski masks down over their whiskered faces from under their woolly hats.

The leader then turned Widdowson back round to face him, took away his mobile phone and keys, pushed him back against the wall, took an aerosol out of his tool bag, sprayed the front of his coat and trousers with petrol and waved a cigarette lighter at him.

'Any funny business and this is for you,' he said quietly. 'Understand?'

'Yes. Yes,' Widdowson jabbered, his voice up an octave.

The man turned him back to face the wall. 'Don't move.'

He nodded.

The other robber had meanwhile been throwing hammers at each of the two CCTV cameras positioned high up the wall. He had managed to crash each of the lenses at first lob.

The robbers splashed through the water-covered floor to the open vault.

Suddenly, the bank alarm started. It was a high-pitched bell, so loud that it caused the very floor of the building to vibrate.

Two young male clerks appeared, one out of the vault, one from behind a trolley; they took in the scene with eyebrows raised, mouths wide open.

The gang leader waved the gun at them.

Their hands shot up like Jack-in-the-boxes.

'Over there. Turn round. Face the wall. If you don't want to see blood on that nice white paintwork, keep absolutely still.'

The two men stood next to Widdowson, facing the wall.

The gang leader pulled a cook's clockwork timer out of his pocket, set it for one minute and put it on a shelf in the vault. Then he took two plastic bags from the tool kit, threw one at the other man and the two of them began to fill them with all the used paper money they could see.

Out of the corner his eye, the leader saw Widdowson sidling towards the security door. He pointed the gun in his direction and pulled the trigger. A shot rang out and made a hole in the plaster a foot away from his head.

Widdowson cried out, 'No! No!' His hands shot back up and he froze against the wall.

The two young clerks pressed themselves closer to the wall, their arms stretching upwards and shaking.

Faces with expressions of panic, fear, excitement, but mostly fear appeared at windows in the security door. The constant hum of the buzzer on the door added to the racket and bedlam.

In the vault were shelves and shelves of paper money in cellophane packets. The robbers were selective. Some packets contained euros and various foreign currencies. They chose used sterling notes, in tens and twenties. There were a lot of the new twenty-pound notes: they preferred the old design, but they didn't waste time being choosey.

Suddenly, the bell on the cook's timer rang. The leader picked it up, stuffed it in the bag with the money and turned to his mate. 'Come on,' he yelled.

They screwed tight the necks of the bags, picked up the tool box, looked round to make sure nothing was left behind, rushed over to the rear door of the bank, unlocked it with the keys on Widdowson's bunch and dashed out.

Outside waiting was the counterfeit ambulance, with its rear doors wide open. They threw the sacks and tool boxes in the back and then themselves. Then the vehicle roared away from the bank, siren wailing as they pulled the doors to from the inside.

'You wanted me, sir?'

'Yes. Come in,' Harker said, looking meaner than usual. His ginger eyebrows fluttered up and down as he spoke. It frequently happened when he didn't understand something or was unusually surprised. He was waving a paper in his hand.

Angel recognized it as his short account of yesterday's events.

'I've read your report. It doesn't make any sense. You have to write reports that make sense.'

Angel sighed. For the first time in his life, he realized that Harker's head looked like a Neolithic skull with ears, nose and chin added as an afterthought.

'What exactly—'

'You've got down here that the man who shot this scrap dealer, Pleasant, was in his bare feet.'

'That's right, sir.'

'Well there you are. I mean, that can't be right. How could he get around? I mean, well, firstly, how could he get to the position on the side of the road to shoot the scrap dealer and then make good his escape? If he had no shoes on, how could he run? And how could he possibly drive? It's almost unknown for us to get a killer by use of a firearm who does not make his or her escape on foot or by means of a road vehicle?'

'I only reported what I found, sir. I can't yet explain—'

'Have you tried walking on pavements and streets without shoes and socks on?'

Angel shook his head.

'It's bad enough trying to walk across the sands. Those sun-baked corrugated surfaces … and pebbles and sea shells play havoc with your instep.'

'Yes, sir.'

'Had you considered that if this outlandish theory was correct, which I don't believe for one moment, then the killer could be used to walking about without shoes?'

'You mean like a native of some foreign country?'

'The Blackfoot were members of a tribe of Algonquin American Indians. I believe they walked about bare foot.'

Angel blinked. 'That was years ago.'

'Might run in the family. Or could it have been a Sasquatch?'

'Sasquatch? Not sure if they really exist, sir.'

He frowned. Harker was getting carried away. Angel couldn't imagine a seven foot ape-like character committing a murder in the backstreets of Bromersley in broad daylight.

'Anyway, they're native to America and have huge feet,' he said. 'But I will keep all my options open, sir.'

'I should hope so.'

'It's early days,' Angel said. 'I certainly have enough evidence to prove that the murderer, at the time of the murder, was standing in his bare feet. That's all I know.'

'Ah! But that isn't the entire story, is it? There's more, isn't there? You go on to say that the murdered man, who is fully dressed in a lounge suit, found dead in the driving seat of a Bentley, has no shoes on! No shoes on. Could he possibly have driven the car there in his stocking feet? And he lived on Creesforth Road. I don't think he could have driven that far in his stocking feet.'

'I am puzzled by it, sir, but I have only just started. I have a good footprint of the murderer. If an appropriately qualified suspect's bare foot matches that footprint, then we have irrefutable evidence that will certainly convict him.'

Harker nodded in confirmation, which made Angel look up in surprise. Harker didn't usually agree with anything he said.

The phone rang. Harker snatched it up.

It was a civilian telephonist in the operations room. She sounded unusually agitated. 'Just received a call from the manager of the control room of Bex Security in Sheffield, sir. They have received a signal indicating an unidentifiable interruption to normality at one of the clients they monitor in Bromersley, namely The Great Northern Bank. They also said that all the banks phone lines are down, and that their fax and computer contacts are dead. Bex are therefore formally advising us that a bank raid is now in progress.'

Harker felt his heart begin to thump. 'Right, I—'

'One moment, sir, please hold on. Something just coming in … in connection with that … ah, my colleague tells me she has received a call from the actual manager of the bank, a Mr Hobson. He confirms that all their lines are down and says he's been able to make contact because he is using his personal mobile phone. He would like to speak to a senior police officer. Shall I patch him through to you?'

Harker licked his lips. He was anxious to take some action. He wasn't certain what. 'Yes, of course.'

The caller's voice was strained.

'Hello? This is Hobson here. I am the manager of The Great Northern Bank.'

'Yes sir, go ahead. Detective Superintendent Harker here.'

Harker could hear the bank alarm screeching through the earpiece.

'We have just had an armed robbery, and the robbers have stolen a great deal of the bank's money!'

CHAPTER 6

Angel and the SOCO team led by DS Taylor arrived to find the Great Northern Bank in chaos and disorder.

A few people were hanging around the front door, which was closed and locked. Customers had been asked to leave. Water was still pouring out of the staff lavatory and the hideous indescribable stink pervaded the entire building.

Angel soon found the source of the smell. It was actually outside the lavatory. Tacked by sticky tape in the hinge of the door was the remains of a small glass vial of what he guessed had contained sulphretted hydrogen. That's what would have created the foul smell. It was simple to trigger. All that had been required was for the lavatory door to be closed. That would have smashed the vial and released the smell. Easy.

Angel was still there at half past four after having surveyed the scene, interviewed the manager, all the staff and taken their written statements. He had worked out most of the details of how the raiders had perpetrated the devious scheme to rob the bank, although he had not yet established how they had managed to arrange for a flood of water to envelop the bank some minutes after the 'pregnant' woman had been taken away in the counterfeit ambulance. The plumbers said that the smell was in no way associated with the water closet or the drains, which were not blocked and had not been blocked throughout the mayhem. The flood, which had consisted of clean, cold water had been caused by some mysterious interference with the ball cock mechanism causing the cistern to overflow ten minutes after the phoney ambulance had taken the woman away. They were unable to provide any explanation as to how the robbers had organized the sophisticated delay and the ensuing flood so skilfully.

SOCO had searched throughout the areas where the raiders had been, but they had not been able to find any fingerprints, footprints, DNA or any other physical evidence. The shell case from the spent bullet was a .32 calibre; it was too common a calibre to be certain of the gun that it was fired from, also there were no prints on the shell case.

Angel had commandeered all the CCTV tapes throughout the bank for that day and hastily raced through them in one of the bank's offices. He observed that the ID of the two male raiders was not going to be possible as they both wore real or false beards during the time they were in the banking hall and then masks in addition when in the secure area. He noticed also that they wore rubber gloves. The CCTV pictures of the 'pregnant' woman were clear, but females were notoriously able to disguise their appearance with wigs and make-up, and the padding stuffed up the young woman's skirt totally camouflaged her physical outline. Her thumb tip and fingertips must have been covered with glued pads because no fingerprints were found on the places she had touched, such as the door and handle of the loo. He made a rough estimation of her height at about five feet four inches.

He trawled the street outside the bank, and ventured into the solicitor's office next door, but no one could give a useful description of the man in the telephone engineer's rig-out, seated on the little stool on Huddersfield Road, who had managed so expertly to intercept and manipulate the various telephone calls to and from the bank and then, before leaving, to assist the gang in its escape, had managed to sever all the bank's telephone and internet links to the outside world. No one seemed to have noticed him and his illicit shenanigans. The presence of a man dressed like that, working at an outside communication box in the street, was such a common sight these days.

Two local bank directors had arrived post haste from Nottingham. They took over the bank from Hobson, interviewed him and sent him home. Their principal tasks had been to cooperate with the police in their investigation to find the raiders, to consider what changes, if any, ought to be made to maintain the highest level of security, determine the branch's losses and get the bank in order for reopening as soon as possible. Under their direction, bank staff, plumbers, carpenters, locksmiths, cleaners, alarm and telephone engineers rushed round the building trying to get the bank organized and ready for re-opening the following morning.

Angel went up to the open door of the manager's office and spoke to one of the directors busy at the desk.

'My chaps have finished here, Mr Benson. And I am off. Have you worked out how much money they took?'

'I have it exactly.' He reached out to an adding machine print out and said, 'Four million, nine hundred thousand pounds sterling. Mostly in used ten and twenty-pound notes. Not bad for a morning's work, eh?' he said wryly.

Angel shook his head. 'Not good,' he said.

'Have you any suspects then?' Benson said.

'No, not yet,' Angel said. He tried to sound bright and optimistic, but privately he reckoned it was going to take some solving. It was a very thoroughly thought out operation. Some person or persons with an understanding of modern telephone technology as well as a master of organization, discipline and simple psychology had conceived this bold plan that had left behind no forensic for him to work on.

'You discovered the source of the foul smell and how it was activated, but did you manage to work out how they managed to flood the place ten minutes after the woman had left the premises?' Benson said.

Angel pursed his lips. 'No, but I hope to.'

'These thieves could have taught Houdini a few tricks, eh?'

Angel sniffed then nodded thoughtfully.

Ahmed opened the door. 'Good morning, sir. You wanted me?'

'Yes, lad,' Angel said. 'Come in. Close the door a minute.'

Ahmed's eyes narrowed as he came up to Angel's desk.

'In the SOCO office,' Angel said, 'Don Taylor has got the lads there making copies in plaster of Paris of the print of the bare foot of the murderer of Charles Pleasant. They're for distribution to the Head of CID at all forty-three forces. It's important that they arrive speedily and in perfect condition. Now I'll give you the draft of a letter to accompany each of them. I want you to print copies of the letter, then liaise with SOCO, and pack them, include a copy of the letter, label them, and get them posted ASAP. All right?'

'Yes, sir,' Ahmed said.

'And tell Don I want a couple of extra copies for me in here, and I want another for our charge room. I'll brief the duty sergeant in the charge room myself, and he can pass it on to the afternoon shift and so on. All right?'

'Right, sir,' he said and bounced cheerfully out of the office.

Angel watched the door close, then looked down at the pile of envelopes on his desk. Most of them had arrived while he had been out of the office the previous day. He fingered through them disinterestedly with a faraway look about him. Then his fingers stopped moving. His mind was on a blurred male figure, at the side of the road, on Sebastopol Terrace, standing there in bare feet, firing a gun. He couldn't stop himself from repeatedly asking why anyone would choose to remove their shoes and socks in order to commit a murder. It had no merit that he could see. It was simply not a good idea, unless the murderer was used to walking bare foot. If that had been so, he would have to consider whether he was looking for someone who didn't need shoes to walk about or drive a car. But that didn't seem right either, because in this country, a barefooted man would be so conspicuous. Nobody could walk the streets of Bromersley without shoes.

His thoughts dissolved away as he realized that someone was knocking at the door.

It was Doctor Mac. He was carrying a large, tightly stuffed Manila envelope with the word EVIDENCE printed in red across it.

Angel smiled at his old friend.

'I finished the PM last night,' Mac said. 'I still have the report to tidy up and print out, but I wanted to get rid of this money. The mortuary doesnae have a safe, you know.' He slapped the thick envelope on Angel's desk.

Angel frowned. He picked up the envelope. It was certainly bulky. 'What's in here?'

'The contents of the victim's pockets including eight thousand quid in twenties, tenners and fivers.'

Angel's eyebrows shot up.

'The money was spread about his pockets,' Mac continued, 'so that it wouldn't stick out too much, I suppose.'

'Is his wallet there?'

'Yes, with more than a hundred quid in it, and there was a parcel of that cash in the same pocket, keeping it company.'

'So our murderer's motive wasn't robbery then,' Angel said. 'Ta, Mac. What else can you tell me that's interesting?'

'Nothing much. He was shot in quick succession, I expect … in the head, twice … then once in the arm and once in the chest. A .32 … from between ten and fifty yards. He would have died instantly.'

'Must have used a silencer?'

Mac nodded. 'Aye. I'm not much into ballistics, but I know with a modern silencer it would have made less noise than the backfiring of a kid's motorbike.'

'Hmm. Was it a handgun?'

'I think so. If it was a handgun, it was well aimed. No wide shots. The one in his arm went straight through him and then out through the windscreen.'

'Any prints on the shell cases?'

'No.'

'Hmm. What sort of a health was he in.'

'Pretty good fettle. Early signs of cirrhosis. Not much. He must have been taking plenty of water with it. Everything else looked in good order. Looked after himself. Probably a member of a gym. Signs of a deep natural tan wearing off. He probably wintered in a hot climate somewhere. His clothes were of the best. Reid and Taylor worsted suit, silk underwear, monogrammed shirt.'

Angel smiled. 'He doesn't sound like your regular scrap-metal man, does he? Was he into drugs?'

'Not as far as I could see. No needle marks … well, not in the usual places anyway. And no tattoos.'

He stood up and made for the door. 'I must go. I'll email the full PM report to you later today.'

'Well thanks, Mac. Must ask you. Can you possibly understand why a murderer would stand in the street in his bare feet to shoot his victim? I mean, have you any idea at all?'

'I have no idea, Michael. I was thinking about it last night. I have absolutely no idea. I'm a scientist. I deal in facts. My investigations produce specific answers. With me, it's yes or no. Positive or negative. Black or white. Fortunately, I don't have those kind of peculiar puzzles to solve. You're the expert there, sorry.'

Angel looked at him and frowned.

Mac went out and closed the door.

Angel rubbed his chin. He didn't feel much of an expert. He reached out and tipped the contents of Pleasant's pockets out of the evidence envelope on to the desk. As well as the big wodge of £8,000 in mixed notes, there were the more usual things: handkerchief, some coins, a soft camel-skin wallet and a five-lever key on its own. He quickly reached out for the key and sighed with satisfaction. He looked at it closely, turned it over, turned it back, there were no marks on it at all. He held one end between finger and thumb, tapped the other end in the palm of his other hand and looked away through the window. It looked as if it might fit the Philip's safe he had discovered in the scrapyard under the forklift. He put the key in his pocket and amended the inventory on the paper stapled to the envelope. Then he reached out for the wallet. Inside there was £120 in notes, plastic cards from all sorts of organizations, including the AA, the Great Northern Bank, and some other lesser known names. He had a few business cards of his own describing the business as metal recovery experts, and that was all.

He put the wallet and everything else except the key back in the envelope, sealed it down with an abundance of Sellotape and rang for Ahmed.

'Take that down to the office. See who is on duty. Ask him to put it in the safe for me and get a receipt. Got it?'

'Right, sir.' Ahmed went out as Gawber came in.

'Have you a minute, sir?'

Angel noticed that Gawber's eyes were shining.

'What is it, Ron?'

'You won't believe it, sir?'

'Try me.'

'Well, you told me to see what I could find out about the two Frazer sisters, Bridie and Jazmin.'

'Yes. Shut the door and sit down. What about them?'

'They were from a respectable family in Skiptonthorpe. Bridie, the elder sister, was a teacher in a school there. Very smartly turned out lass. Happily married, or so it seemed, in 1978 to a quiet, hard-working lad called Larry Longley, a butcher. They had one son, Abe Longley. However, over the years, Bridie got to know a man who had a transport business. He had a fleet of wagons doing long haul, mostly taking steel billets from Sheffield up to Glasgow then bringing whisky back and delivering it to a warehouse in the Isle of Dogs in London. Well, the relationship got what you might call hot, and Bridie was having it off with this chap. In return, he was buying her expensive designer clothes and handbags, jewellery and taking her away on foreign holidays and stuff. They were flying really high. The thing is, the husband knew all about it. In fact, he used to look after the son, young Abe, sometimes while his wife and this chap went off together. More than one occasion he took his young son away, when they went away somewhere different.'

'Yes. I remember some of this coming out in court. Nasty set up, the whole thing. But Bridie got too greedy, didn't she?'

'Yes sir. The boyfriend couldn't keep up with the money. He wouldn't or couldn't stump up for something she wanted, so they had an unholy row, and she walked out on him. She went back to her husband and their son. Later that day the boyfriend came to the Longleys' house looking for her. Larry Longley said she was out with young Abe. He pushed past him into the house and searched it. Larry saw red and went after him with a poker. The boyfriend pushed him away and stormed out of the house. Two days later Bridie's body was found in an oil drum, chopped up in pieces. An AA man tried to move the drum off the hard shoulder of the A1 in Leicestershire and discovered the body.'

Angel pulled a face. 'The husband got sent down, didn't he?'

'He got twenty years, sir. The chopper used on Bridie was the same chopper he used to use for cutting up stewing steak in the butcher's shop. He's doing time in Wakefield prison.'

'Has he appealed?'

'Twice. Each time it was rejected. And this is the bit you won't believe, sir. When the boyfriend walked out of Longley's house, he went straight to Jones's antique shop and enticed Jazmin Jones, Bridie's sister, away from her husband, Emlyn Jones. Then Jazmin Jones changed her name back to her maiden name, Frazer.'

Angel nodded and took over the story. 'Charles Pleasant and Jazmin Frazer were at Larry's trial, holding hands. They were together throughout the trial and have been together ever since … until his murder on Sunday.'

Gawber's face dropped. 'You knew, sir!'

'Not all of it.'

'Yes. His father died in 2003 and left him the scrap metal business. Shortly afterwards Charles sold the haulage business for a tidy sum.'

'He must have been pretty well off then?'

'Not for long. Not while either of the Frazer sisters were anywhere around.'

Gawber smiled.

'What do you know about Bridie and Larry's son?'

'Information about him is a bit sparse. I worked out that Abe must be 28.'

His eyebrows shot up. 'Doesn't time fly?'

Gawber nodded pensively.

'When you've time, I want you to find him,' Angel said, but at that moment, his mind was on a more pressing matter. He delved into his pocket and pulled out the key he had taken from Pleasant's evidence envelope. He waved it at him. 'In the meantime, there is a more pressing matter. I may have the key that will open the safe in the scrapyard. You'd better come with me.'

Angel drove the car straight into the scrapyard at the end of Sebastopol Terrace and parked behind SOCO's van.

Taylor saw Angel and Gawber arrive and came out of the little office. He was still in the white overalls. He threw up a salute and said: 'Good morning, sir.'

'Good morning, Don.' Angel looked at him hopefully. 'Found anything interesting?'

'Afraid not, sir. We're about finished here. Going to do the grates both here and in the street and then we're away.'

'Move that forklift so that we can get to the safe, will you? I think I have the key for it.'

Taylor's face brightened. 'Right, sir,' he said and he jumped up on the forklift and drove it forward ten feet or so.

Angel pushed the steel sheet away, crouched down, and put the key in the safe lock. He knew instantly it was the right one. He smiled as he felt and heard the solid click.

Taylor and Gawber leaned forward. They all peered expectantly as he turned the brass handle and lifted up the heavy door.

But the safe was empty.

All they saw was the scuffed and dusty yellow-painted lining with an old-fashioned logo around the name 'Philips'. The three men became very quiet.

Angel stood up, rubbed his chin, turned to Taylor and said: 'Check this out, Don. See if you can determine what Pleasant had last hidden in here.'

'I'll do what I can, sir.'

Angel dropped Gawber off at the station, collected a cardboard shoe box from Ahmed and then drove the BMW down to the town centre on to Victoria Street to the car park at the back of the NHS clinic. He parked the BMW and walked round to the front entrance carrying the shoe box under his arm. Through the door facing him there were lots of signs with long medical words on them. He picked out the one he wanted and went over to a pretty young lady at a desk.

'I phoned earlier. My name is DI Angel. I'm from Bromersley police.'

The young lady in the blue uniform smiled. 'Oh yes,' she said. 'Doctor May has just arrived. Please go to treatment room number two over there. He's expecting you.'

'Thank you.'

He knocked on the door and opened it.

A young man in a white coat was sitting at a desk going through some papers.

'Doctor May?'

'Come in,' he said smiling. 'You must be the famous Inspector Angel?' he said. He closed the file of papers and got to his feet.

Angel shook his head and pulled a face. He wasn't used to compliments. He certainly didn't feel famous. Genuine compliments were about the only thing that made him stuck for words.

'No,' he muttered, 'just plain Inspector Angel.'

Then he quickly held up the cardboard box and removed the lid. 'You said you would kindly look at a footprint.'

'Anything I can do to assist the police, of course.'

He passed the box containing the plaster cast to the young doctor.

'What can you tell me about this, Doctor?'

Doctor May put the box on the desk and looked down at it.

'There's not much to go on, I fear, Inspector.'

Angel licked his lips. 'We came across this footprint at the scene of a crime. Please tell me whatever you can?'

'What occurs to me firstly is that it seems to be a perfectly healthy foot. There is nothing actually wrong with it. No signs of any past surgery either.'

'Is it male or female?'

'Judging by the size and contraction of the toes, I would say probably male.'

He pursed his lips. Probably? Up to that point, Angel had been positive that it had been the print of a man's foot.

'Why only probably male?'

'The main differences between a male and a female foot in the Western world is that the male is larger, but the toes are more likely to be contracted, while the female foot is more likely to spend more time in open-toed shoes, sandals or no shoes at all. The female toes would therefore be less likely to be contracted. This wasn't the case early last century, but these things change.'

'Are the toes in this footprint contracted?'

'They are partly contracted, which suggests that it is the footprint of a man who has historically worn close-fitting Western-type shoes. Also his big toe is not enlarged as it would be if he walked bare foot a lot.'

'So, does this man regularly wear Western-type shoes today?'

‘Probably.’

Angel sighed. He was hoping for a word like, ‘Yes’, or ‘No’. ‘Probably’ wasn’t much help. He thought a moment and then said. ‘Tell me, Doctor, in your experience and speaking generally, is the only reason that people walk about in bare feet because they can’t afford shoes? Or is that an oversimplification?’

Doctor May smiled. ‘I believe that most of the people of the world would want to wear shoes if they could afford them. Does that answer your question?’

‘Yes, Doctor, thank you. But what’s your last word about the man who made this footprint then?’

‘If I was to stick my neck out, I would say that the foot that made this mark has worn Western-type shoes all his life.’

‘And how old do you think the man might be?’

‘Very difficult. It’s a fully grown foot, so the minimum age I would say would be about sixteen or seventeen. The maximum is much more difficult. The foot shows no sign of degeneration or muscle relapse, so it is probably somebody in their twenties or thirties, but depending on the person’s lifestyle, he could be as old as fifty or sixty or even sixty-five. Sorry I cannot be more help.’

‘You’ve assisted me more than you know, Doctor. Thank you very much.’

CHAPTER 7

Angel looked at his watch. It was a few minutes past twelve o'clock. He licked his lips. He was thirsty. He could just sink a pint.

He drove the BMW back up to the police station car park, parked it up and then walked down to the Fat Duck. It was the nearest pub to the station and was a frequent haunt of his at lunchtimes.

He pushed open the door and looked round. The bar was as inviting as usual: the brass and glass were shining pleasingly. But it wasn't busy. There was nobody at the tables, and only two old men standing at the bar. He recalled times when the place would have been heaving with customers. He sniffed. That new 'no smoking' in public places law was going to annihilate the British pub. A pretty girl appeared behind the bar. She greeted him and flashed a smile making it easy to reciprocate.

'A glass of Old Peculier, please,' he said. 'And a meat pie.'

He thanked her, passed her a fiver, she rang it up in the till, and then dropped a few coins in his hand. He moved to a cosy table by the window.

The beer was chilled and tasted good.

He was enjoying the peace and quiet and thinking about what the doctor had said when a man he hadn't noticed before and didn't know came across to him. He was a burly man about 40 years of age, he was wearing a dark suit, white vest and leather shoes, and he had several heavy gold chains round his neck. He was carrying a glass of beer.

'Detective Inspector Angel, isn't it?'

Angel looked up, nodded and continued chewing the pie. The man spoke good English but he wasn't local. Possibly foreign.

'May I join you?'

Angel would have wished that he wouldn't, there were twenty or more other unoccupied tables, but he wasn't inclined to be churlish.

'Yes. Sure.'

The man banged the glass on to the table, spilling a little, he noticed, but looked unconcerned and sat down opposite him.

Angel didn't like him. He wondered what he wanted. He was uncomfortable with his proximity. He started to observe the little things. He noticed he had big hands with clean fingernails and that the nails had a regular spade shape. Here was a man who could afford a manicure. He was wearing an Oré gold watch on a heavy gold bracelet and a gold signet ring. He obviously knew how to spend money. As Angel swallowed a mouthful of pie and licked his lips, he wondered how the man had earned it. He was still thinking about that as he glanced round the bar and realized that the two old men and the barmaid weren't there anymore. There were just the two of them in the room. Something was not quite normal. It should be busier and noisier. He raised his head.

Then the man leaned over the table until he was only six inches away from Angel's nose. 'You've got something of mine,' he said quietly. 'And I want it.'

Angel felt his pulse begin to bang away. He stared into the man's mean, little eyes. He carefully clocked his face. He hadn't seen the man before. He took his time. He shrugged and said, 'If it's yours, you shall certainly have it. What's your name?'

'Just call me Gold.'

Angel had never heard of him. 'Right, Mr Gold.'

'Just Gold. The thing is, you have moved it, and I want to know where you have moved it to?'

'What are we talking about?'

'Don't come that,' he sneered. 'You are the DI Angel of Bromersley nick, aren't you. Got a reputation for always getting your man, because you got second sight or you've got a computer for a brain or something. That is you, isn't it?'

He hesitated, frowned and then said: 'I am DI Angel of Bromersley police. There is nobody else there by that name.'

Alarm bells began to sound in his head. Gold's attitude suggested that he had some back-up or support of some kind close by. He decided to test it before the crosstalk went any further. He finished the pie, emptied the glass, wiped his mouth with the miniscule serviette that had been under the pie, and stood up. 'If you care to make an appointment to see me at the station, I will try to assist you. Now I must go.'

Gold smiled. 'Sit down, Inspector.'

Angel's eyes widened. He could hear his pulse bang louder in his ears. 'I haven't time.'

He turned towards the door.

Gold stood up. 'All right, I'll come with you,' he said. Then he put two fingers across his front teeth, screwed up his mouth and let out a piercing whistle.

The saloon bar door opened and two huge men were standing there. They must have been there some time. They were in dark suits and wore sunglasses. Their coats bulged under their breast pockets.

Angel knew he was in serious trouble. He had never seen either of them in person before, nor were they in the station picture gallery.

'The Inspector wants to leave, Shadrack,' he said. 'We are giving him a lift to the nick,' he said with a grin. 'On the way, he's going to talk to us.'

'I don't know what you want,' Angel said. 'I can easily walk there. It isn't far.'

The two men in sunglasses separated, allowing Angel to walk between them. He strode out boldly between them. It was never wise to show how afraid you were, but three armed men to one unarmed man were odds he didn't care for. He was thinking that these were not a local mob. He strode between them to the door, but when outside, they gently but firmly bundled him into a car. He was pushed into the middle seat in the back. He clocked that it was a dark blue Ford.

Gold was last in. He sat next to him and closed the door. Shadrack got into the driver's seat. The third man got into the car from the nearside back door and squashed up next to him. He was very close. There was a sickly smell of cheap Armenian brandy.

'This isn't necessary,' Angel protested. 'What is it you want?'

'Let's go the scenic route,' Gold said.

'I have to return to my office,' Angel said.

The driver pulled out of the Fat Duck car park and headed along Huddersfield Road out of the town.

Gold turned to Angel and said, 'Now then, Inspector, you're getting a free lift. Well, it's not exactly free. The charge is simply information. What have you done with the head. It's mine and I want it back.'

'I have no idea what you are talking about, Mr Gold.'

'Just Gold. You're the copper investigating the death of Charles Pleasant, aren't you?'

'Yes.'

'Well don't mess me about. As you will know, he had the jade head of Hang Mung Cheng. I want it.'

Angel frowned. That was the head mentioned in the paper. Stolen from some foreign country. Worth millions. This man looked as if he would kill for it.

'I was not aware of that,' he said calmly.

'Don't mess me about,' Gold yelled. 'You must have found it. It was at Pleasant's scrapyard.'

'No, it wasn't. There was a safe hidden there but it was empty. I didn't know what it was supposed to contain. I found the key yesterday and opened it, and it was empty.'

Gold gasped. 'It couldn't have been. Pleasant arranged to sell it to me before he died. We agreed a price. Twenty thousand pounds. I've got the money. You can have it. Cash. No questions asked. You have got it. You must have it. What have you done with it?'

'I have never even seen it.'

Gold's face was scarlet, his eyes sticking out. 'You've taken it and hidden it away somewhere for a rainy day.'

'I assure you I wouldn't dream of such a thing. I can only tell you that I was not alone when the safe was opened. There were two other men present. They would tell you exactly what I have told you, that the safe was empty.'

This seemed to surprise Gold.

'What? Who?' he said, then he added, 'Coppers?'

'One of them was.'

'You coppers stick as close as blood to a blanket.'

'One of the men *wasn't* in the force. He worked for Pleasant. He was there when the safe was opened. I assure you there was nothing in it, nothing at all.'

'You're lying, Angel. You found the safe and opened it – probably in the night – took the head and hid it somewhere. You're just play-acting.'

'I didn't, and I wouldn't. I didn't get the key until yesterday morning. Before then, it was locked away with the body in the mortuary. I didn't know the key existed or that the safe existed or indeed that there was any question that a jade head you speak of might have been concealed in it. Nor did any other person – that I know of – have the slightest inkling. That can all be proved. It's on the record.'

'Not "a" jade head,' Gold said. 'Not any old chuffing jade head, but "the" only jade head in the world,' he snarled. 'I am not playing for ha'pennies, Angel.' Then he seemed to have a thought. He rubbed his chin. He was quiet for a few moments.

Angel noticed that the car passed the speed restriction signs out of Bromersley. They were passing fields and trees. Shadrack had put his foot down on the accelerator. Every minute was a mile further away from Bromersley.

After a few moments, Gold spoke in a more measured tone. 'Who else was with you when you opened it?'

'DS Gawber, and an employee of Charles Pleasant, Grant Molloy. But I am sure they know nothing about it. I assure you, I didn't know anything about it until you mentioned it.'

He hardened again. 'Angel, you'd better not be fooling me. I know it is around here somewhere. I have to find it.'

Gold then tapped the driver on the shoulder and said, 'Shadrack, pass me that tape, then turn round somewhere convenient and stop.'

Shadrack nodded and over his shoulder passed him a roll of brown sticky plastic tape about two inches wide.

'Have you got any children, Angel?' Gold said.

'Not yet, why?'

'If I find you've been frigging me around, I'll find you, wherever you are, and I'll make certain that if ever your wife ever hears the patter of tiny feet in your house, it'll be mice. Understand?'

Angel had to nod.

He vowed that if he escaped with his life, he would do everything he could to get him behind bars.

'Put your hands behind your back,' Gold said.

'Is there really any need for this?' Angel said. He had no idea what was planned for him. He glanced out of the window. He tried to get his bearings. They were out in the country in the middle of nowhere. There was just open road, fields, and not a building in sight.

Gold wrapped about a foot of tape around his wrists, then tore it off with his teeth. He then wound it several times round his head covering his eyes.

Angel couldn't see a thing. He was really angry. 'This really isn't necessary!' he yelled.

Gold wrinkled his nose, 'If I didn't do this, I don't know what you'd get up to, being the smart-arsed detective you're supposed to be.'

'This is outrageous!'

'And if you don't shut it,' Gold added, 'I'll put this stuff over that fat mouth of yours as well.'

The car slowed and then stopped.

Gold got out. 'Come on, you bastard copper,' he said dragging him out of the back seat. 'You had better have been telling the truth or I'll be back to finish you off.' He then pushed him into the middle of the highway.

Angel heard the car door close and the car drive off at speed. He breathed heavily with relief, but realized he was on the highway and potentially in the way of road traffic. He staggered, taking a few paces in every direction until he found a kerb, tripped over it, picked himself up, and was relieved to find a grassy surface where he managed to fall down. His shoulders hurt and his wrists were being cut into by the tape. He rolled on to his side and listened. There was the distant hum of traffic, he sensed that would be coming from the M1 which might have been about three miles away, the rustle of leaves touching each other in the gentle breeze, and then intermittently, the twitter of a bird accompanied by the sound it made when diving through the air to play or in its search for food.

Several vehicles raced past but either didn't see him or ignored him. He eventually heard footsteps running towards him. He listened, then when he thought the runner was close, he called out, 'I am a police officer. Will you please remove this tape from my eyes and undo my wrists?'

The footsteps slowed, stopped and there was a pause.

Angel listened attentively, then repeated his plea.

A panting voice said: 'What you doing like this mate? Was it for a bet?'

The man peeled the tape from over his eyes.

The runner was in the gear: shorts, trainers and sweatshirt.

Angel blinked. 'Oh thank you so much.'

The young man laughed and unfastened his wrists.

'Some people would do anything for a laugh,' he said.

'Thank you. Thank you very much.'

'Anytime,' the young man said with a grin and continued his run.

Angel reached in his pocket for his mobile and tapped in a number.

Gawber soon replied and sighed with relief. 'Wow. We've been worried about you, sir,' Gawber said. 'The landlord at The Fat Duck phoned in to say that he'd been held at the end of a gun in his cellar, and his barmaid had been locked in an airing cupboard by two men who had followed you into the snug. Then they left, and when he came up and looked in the bar, so had you. The bar was empty. He put two and two together and phoned us. We have had four cars standing by, but we had no idea where to send them.'

Angel appreciated it, but he would have done no less for Gawber and any other member of his team.

'I'm all right. Come and collect me. I'm on the main Bromersley to Huddersfield road, about half-way between Cheviton and Lower Springfield.'

'On my way, sir. I'll put out a look out notice for their car, if you can give me the index number.'

'It was a big, dark blue Ford, Ron. That's all I got. They were far too clever for me.'

Twenty minutes later, Gawber picked up Angel from the country road and they returned together to the station in his car.

'Phew! I don't want that to happen again,' Angel said when they were back in his office. 'Chief thug was a man who told me his name. Said it was Gold. I've not heard of him. And one of the heavies he called Shadrack.'

Gawber shook his head. 'Don't ring any bells with me, and they're the sort of names you'd remember.'

Angel nodded. 'Get me the up-to-date video of national mug shots, will you. I'll look at them on my lap top. Might recognize somebody.'

'Right, sir,' he said and went out.

Angel sighed. There was just too much to do. He must deal with the priorities. It's when you're overworked you tend to work at the job in front of you and permit yourself to deal with events as they come up instead of working to a sensible, proven sequence and sticking to it. Everything that drops in your lap you think you can deal with quickly, but it is time consuming and some of it is not urgent. Everybody else thinks that their time is important, and it is, to them, but not to the investigation of the murder of Charles Pleasant. Murder was always his first priority and he must stick to the orderly examination of the evidence, and he must do it while it was still hot. He hadn't yet heard from SOCO. He must see what was happening there, and he must go back to the crime scene.

The phone rang. He glared at it and muttered a rude word. He had wanted to phone Taylor and chase up the results of their search of the crime scene. He reached out for it and snatched it up. It was DS Matthew Elliott at the Antiques and Fine Art squad, London. He was an old friend of his and they had worked on many cases together over the years. He couldn't brush him off.

After they had exchanged pleasant greetings, Elliott said, 'I'll tell you why I'm phoning. You've no doubt heard about the missing jade head of this famous oriental chap, Hang Mung Cheng? Well, I have some information that it is in your neck of the woods. The information that has come down is that it is in the possession of a scrap dealer, of all people, a Charles Pleasant in Bromersley. Is he known to you?'

Angel's head shot up. 'Not in the sense you mean, Matthew. He is known to us, because he was murdered on Sunday afternoon last. Four gun shots in broad daylight.'

There was a pause. Elliott was clearly surprised. 'I suppose the murderer got away with the jade head?'

'I don't know. We haven't got that far. We haven't found it. Could be your information is out of date … or late, if you see what I mean.'

He told him all the pertinent facts of the case and in particular surprised him when he told him that the murderer of Pleasant had been a man in bare feet, and also that the victim himself had been found without shoes.

'I don't understand the idiosyncrasies of people with homicidal tendencies, Michael. Their interest in bare feet and shoes is too difficult for me to comprehend. All I know is that I'm under a lot of pressure to find this jade head. I am being hammered by my boss. He's had a phone call from the Home Secretary and a personal appeal from the Empress of Xingtunanistan, Louise Elizabeth Mung Cheng, the woman who is the rightful owner. There is desperate heat on to find it and get it back undamaged. Apart from political prestige, it's worth millions! Where can I go from here?'

'You're not the only one with that thought.' He related his experience at the hands of Gold, Shadrack and the other heavy.

'I don't know of them, Michael, but every crook and arty person in the world the slightest bit bent is on the look-out for it.'

'Our SOCO team have searched Pleasant's scrapyard, but have still to search his house. They're a bit overwhelmed.'

'I'll come up. I'll be there first thing in the morning.'

'All right, Matthew. See you then.'

Angel put his hand on the cradle, waited for the line to clear then he dialled a number. It was answered by Taylor.

'Did you check out that empty safe, Don?'

'There was a showing that gold had been in there, sir, but nothing else that I could identify.'

'Any jade?'

'Did you say jade, sir?'

'Yes. Green stone. Comes from China and … out there.'

'I know jade, sir,' Taylor said. 'No, sir. No jade.'

Angel pulled a face. If the jade head had been carefully wrapped it would not necessarily have left behind any trace.

'Did you finish the grates?' he asked.

'Yes sir. All the way up the street. Nothing there.'

He wrinkled his nose. 'Right, Don. Don't suppose you found the shoes?'

'No, sir. No shoes. We're still making moulds of that footprint. Ahmed should get some off tonight. And we hope to get into the victim's house first thing tomorrow.'

'Good.' He replaced the phone.

He sighed. Wouldn't it be great if he could recover Charles Pleasant's shoes? He couldn't believe that the man left the house in his stocking feet. What would be the point? Assuming that he was wearing shoes when he left home, a perfectly proper and logical assumption, then, for whatever reason he must have taken them off and disposed of them sometime between leaving the house, driving to the scrap-yard, opening the gates, returning to the car and getting shot. So the shoes should be somewhere along Creesforth Road, Park Road, Bromersley town centre, Wakefield Road and Sebastopol Terrace, assuming that that was the route he took on that quiet Sunday afternoon. If he could recover the shoes, who knows what forensic they might hold. But how could he find them? He could leaflet the area. Every house, both sides of the road. That would be two or three hundred houses and shops.

'Lost. One pair of black leather shoes, size nine.'

He rubbed his chin and looked out of the window. The more he thought about it, the dafter it sounded.

Under average circumstances, partly worn shoes wouldn't have a value. People might wear somebody else's shirt or vest or dress or whatever. Buy it at a jumble sale or somewhere, wash it and put it on. But they were unlikely to buy secondhand shoes. They hardly had a value in this country. They'd simply be dumped.

If the shoes had been – for whatever reason – thrown out of the car window, they might have been collected by a street-cleaner, shoved in a bin and disposed of.

Street cleaner! There was a thought.

He picked up the phone and summoned Ahmed.

'I want you to find out who cleans the streets. It'll be a council department. Highways Cleansing or something like that. They'll tell you who is in charge of it at the town hall. Go down and see him. See if any of the men who actually clean the streets, particularly in the town centre, have come across any shoes over the past couple of days. They would be black leather, elasticated sides, size nine and in good fettle.'

'Right, sir.'

CHAPTER 8

It was six o'clock. Angel looked up from his desk. He arched his back then straightened up and stretched it. He sighed. It had been one of those days. He usually finished at five, but there was so much paperwork. He didn't want to be suffocated in the stuff. He wanted to clear his desk so that he could give full attention to the Pleasant case. He gathered the remaining papers on his desk into a pile and slipped them into the top drawer and locked it. He closed the office door, tramped down the quiet green-painted corridor, past the empty cells and out of the rear door. He got in the BMW and had intended going straight home but as he reached the station car park entrance, he slowed the car. He recalled that he had not yet seen Stanley Jones. He had hoped to question him the day previous, but there had not been time. He had also wanted to interview him away from the influence of his father. He knew how inhibiting Emlyn Jones could be; he didn't want him nodding and winking at his son behind his back, and interrupting and prompting the young man at every twist and turn of the questioning. But he was tired. He had had a long day; nevertheless, he made the decision to call on him. He had the address on the back of an envelope in his pocket, so he stopped the car and consulted it: 'Flat 14, Council Close, Potts New Estate, Bromersley.'

He pressed the indicator to the left and let in the clutch.

It was in the better class of council estates on the outskirts of Bromersley; the flats had not been up for very long. Number fourteen was on the ground floor. He rang the bell and waited.

An athletic young man in a vest, jogging trousers and trainers pulled open the door. He had a long nose and sharp chin like a boxer and his hair was shiny black and flat as if it had been stuck down with Cherry Blossom. He spoke with a slight touch of a Welsh accent, boyo, and he stuck out his chin challengingly when he spoke.

'Yes? Oh it's you. Detective Inspector Angel. I remember you. Tried to get me on a shoplifting charge years ago, but you couldn't make it stick. Short on evidence, weren't you? What do you want? My father said you would call. Something to do with my mother's fancy piece, Charles Pleasant. Or should I say ex-fancy piece?'

'Not entirely,' Angel said. 'May I come in? Can we talk somewhere quietly?'

A woman's voice from the inside of the house yelled, 'Stanley! Whoever it is, get shut of them. Your dinner's ready.'

Jones glanced behind him, tightened his lips then said, 'Can't see you now.'

Angel's head came up. His muscles tightened. 'It's very important,' he said. 'We are talking about the death of a man.'

'Won't it do tomorrow?'

Angel licked his lips. 'I can come back in a hour, I suppose.'

Jones hesitated. He looked back along the hall and then at Angel. 'Well, better get it over with, I suppose. Come in,' he snapped.

The house was a jumble of furniture old and new with no special style or care about it at all. He showed Angel into the front room and pointed at a dusty upholstered chair. 'Sit there.' He touched his nose with his forefinger and said, 'I remember, I have just to get something.'

Jones went back out into the hall.

Angel looked round the small room. It was overfull with furniture, three easy chairs, all odd, a TV with a huge screen, and a piano across the back wall with lots of women's clothes draped untidily over it. On top of the clothes bizarrely he saw a solitary parsnip. He stood up, picked it up and looked closely at it to make sure that, indeed, that's what it was. It was a long root. It had been scrubbed clean but not peeled and its top had been neatly cut off. He remembered he had seen a bunch of parsnips, but unwashed and unprepared complete with their green tops, incongruously on the cupboard in his father's, Emlyn Jones's, office. He frowned and then smiled as he wondered if raw parsnips were used in some ritual that he had not yet heard of … something peculiar to the Welsh?

Suddenly he heard banter between Jones and a squawky female. His voice was getting louder. He was coming back.

Angel gasped, quickly banged the parsnip down exactly where he had found it on top of the woman's coat on the piano, and returned to the chair.

Jones came through the door and eyed Angel uncertainly. He was carrying what looked like a sheet of A4 paper with some heavy colouring on the reverse side. He kept it close to his chest turned away so that Angel couldn't see the picture.

'She's a bit upset. Dinner's spoiling. Let's get it over with. What do you want?'

Angel nodded. 'As you obviously know by now, Charles Pleasant was shot dead at his scrapyard on Sunday afternoon. I need to know where your father was at the time.'

Jones's lips curled downwards. 'It was my mother put you up to this wasn't it?'

'An accusation has been made,' he replied trying to stay cool. 'I just have the job of following it up, that's all.'

'My mother has put you up to this though, hasn't she?'

'I don't need or want to get into any of your family disputes, Mr Jones. They are not my business. If you know where your father was on Sunday afternoon, just tell me.'

Stanley Jones turned the A4 sheet of paper over and held it in front of Angel's eyes. 'Here,' he said. 'Take a good look at that. Take it.'

Angel took the sheet of paper. On it was printed a photograph. It was in colour and it showed the head and shoulders close-up of two men, taken from a low angle. Behind them was a clock hanging high up on a wall that showed the time to be 4.30 exactly, and a banner underneath it that read: 'Congratulations to Potts for 20 years security'.

'That was taken at The Feathers Hotel last Sunday afternoon.'

Angel recognized the hotel ballroom. He had been in there many a time. The Police Federation held local meetings there, and he'd been there as a wedding guest not long since. His eyebrows shot up when he saw that the two men, standing side by side, raising champagne glasses, were Emlyn Jones and Detective Superintendent Harker.

Angel stared at the photograph and noted thankfully that Harker was in civvies, and not in uniform, even though it looked like he was wearing an ill-fitting dark suit that he had seen him wear sometimes in the office that had been his grandfather's.

'*I* took that photograph,' Jones said, sticking his chin out. 'Got the original on my computer.' He put his finger on the Superintendent and said, 'And he's one of yours.' He forced a smile and a snigger. 'I spoke to him. He spoke back to me. Not very bright for a copper, though.'

Angel didn't comment. He peered closely at the photograph again. It was printed on regular computer photocopier paper and certainly seemed to be the genuine article.

'Take it. It's yours,' Jones said and ran his hand over his shiny black hair. 'I can give you as many copies of it as you like. Anything else you want to know, Inspector?' he said cockily.

It certainly seemed to be conclusive. It needed checking out with the Superintendent, of course. If it was as genuine as it seemed, neither Emlyn Jones nor his son, Stanley, could have murdered Charles Pleasant.

Holding the paper, Angel stood up. 'That's fine for now,' he said. 'Thank you. That's all I wanted to know.'

Jones smiled at him with his mouth but not with his steely black eyes. He crossed the little room, grabbed hold of the knob and pulled the door open widely.

Angel nodded, slowly crossed over to the doorway and turned.

'Anything else?' Jones snarled.

'No,' Angel said. 'Thank you.' As he spoke, he noticed out of his eye corner that the parsnip that had been on top of the coat on the piano was no longer there. It had mysteriously disappeared. His eyebrows shot up uncontrollably.

It was seven o'clock when Angel arrived home.

Mary Angel was not in her usual pleasant frame of mind.

'I hope you're not going to start coming home at this ridiculous time on a regular basis again,' she said, whilst banging pans, rattling pots and jangling cutlery as if to emphasize her mood. 'Sit down. I couldn't possibly keep your dinner from shrivelling up.'

Angel poured himself a cold German beer straight from the fridge. Then he pulled out a chair and sat down at the kitchen table.

'Couldn't be helped, love.'

'That's what you always say.'

She dropped something dark brown and solid on to a plate.

He thought it clattered on to it like a pair of handcuffs.

'If you can't eat it, I suppose I can do you some eggs.'

He looked at it quizzically. 'It'll be fine.'

She turned back to the oven top and took off a pan lid. She looked inside. 'You wouldn't think so to look at them, but these were boiled potatoes.' She slapped the mush on to his plate. Then returned to the oven top for another pan. She slapped something out of that pan on to his plate.

'What's this?'

'Parsnips.'

He smiled. 'Parsnips!' He shook his head and said, 'I knew it would be.'

'What do you mean? I thought you liked parsnips?'

'I do. I do.'

'Gravy?'

'Ta, love.'

He dug into the meal. The vegetables and gravy were tolerably edible, but the handcuffs were too tough to cut through.

She sat at the table with him sipping a glass of tonic water.

He told her about seeing the bunch of parsnips in Emlyn Jones's office, and the single one in his son Stanley's house, and how in both instances the men had promptly hidden them away from him as if, in some way, they were an illegal substance.

'Maybe they were a bit self-conscious, and thought that it was wrong to have vegetables anywhere but in the kitchen.'

He wrinkled his nose. He didn't think that was the explanation at all.

'Is there anything else useful you can do with a parsnip besides eating it?' he said.

'There's parsnip wine.'

'Ah yes. Potent too, I believe,' he said. But that wasn't the explanation either. He knew human nature. There was something more significant than that.

'Parsnips are not involved in the preparation of medicines are they?'

'I don't imagine so.'

'Or poisons? They don't represent a particular symbol of anything to gypsies or witches or the occult? There are lots of young lasses running round with crystals and amethysts and candles, making all sorts of smells and weird claims. There's apple bobbing—'

Mary looked at him and smiled. 'Michael. A parsnip is simply a vegetable. That's all.'

'I know. I know.'

'I seem to remember something about cutting up carrots and boiling them in water for a long time ... six hours, I think,' she said.

Angel pulled a face.

'You were supposed to drink it ... as a protection against the plague.'

'Yes, but that was carrots and four or five hundred years ago,' he said.

'Well I have no other suggestions, Michael. As I said, a parsnip is simply a vegetable. That's all.'

He nodded but he wasn't convinced. 'The Joneses were up to something, Mary. They may have murdered Pleasant, or they may not. Whatever they were up to somehow, somewhere, in some way, it involved parsnips, or why would they attempt to hide them from me?'

Mary Angel was bored with the subject. She picked up the magazine with the quiz in it.

'There's one I can't do, Michael. You might know it.'

'Yes?'

'What's the collective word for a gathering of crows or ravens?

He knew this from way back. 'A murder,' he said.

Her face brightened.

'That's what I thought,' she said, digging her ballpoint into the magazine.

'What's that all about?'

'It's a quiz in this magazine. The first prize is £50,000.'

He sniffed. 'It would pay the gas bill, anyway.'

'And get me a new coat.'

'And pay the council tax.'

'Dream on.'

Angel arrived at the station the following morning at 8.28 a.m. and went straight up to Superintendent Harker's office, handed him the computer-printed photograph and asked for confirmation that it was indeed a true picture of him standing next to Emlyn Jones.

Harker stared at the picture for a full half minute, while, at the same time sticking a white menthol inhaler up his nostril and sniffing. At length he said: 'Yes. That's Emlyn Jones and that's me, but I hardly exchanged six words with the man throughout the entire afternoon. That photograph must have been taken by young Jones without my noticing. He was flying around the room all the time with a camera, I remember.'

Angel sniffed.

'The Chief Constable thought that someone should accept the invitation from Councillor Potts and attend as an observer,' Harker continued. 'It's as well to know what's going on in the town. I didn't attend Potts's function to be seen to approve or support his business or his friends in any way, you know. I really have no idea how effective Potts's company is. All I know is that I see his annoying little advertising signs of a man in a quasi-police uniform with a German Shepherd dog next to him, fastened to fences and hammered on to doors and gates all over the place.'

'As evidence, it really is quite significant, sir,' Angel said. 'Charles Pleasant's partner, Jazmin, is the mother of Stanley and was once the wife of Emlyn Jones.'

'Mmm. I see the clock shows 1630 hours. The anonymous phone call was timed in at 1625 hours, so the actual moment of death was obviously even earlier than that.'

'Mac was very quickly on the scene. Blood from some of the wounds was not congealed. He agrees the time was around or even a little before 1620.'

'That's near enough. There's no question of Jones, or his son, being able to be at the scrapyard on Sebastopol Terrace at 1620 hours and then back at The Feathers at 1630.'

'No, sir. But I will check up on the accuracy of that ballroom clock.'

Harker's head came up. 'Why?'

'Jones had a powerful motive. I'd like to be absolutely certain. If the clock has been interfered with, it would invalidate Jones's photograph as an alibi, wouldn't it?'

Harker looked up at Angel and blinked. 'Yes, of course.'

CHAPTER 9

There was a knock at the door. It was Ahmed.

'Good morning, sir. I have been to the Highway Cleansing Department on Victoria Street and spoken to the manager. He said that none of the twenty-four cleaners had come across any black leather shoes in the last few days. They come across all sorts of things in their job, including discarded trainers and cheap shoes, usually odd ones, but none of them had come across any black leather shoes as described. However, they said they'd keep looking.'

Angel grunted and wrinkled his nose. It had been a long shot anyway. 'Right.' He couldn't hide his disappointment.

'Sorry, sir,' Ahmed said and turned to go.

'Hang on a minute. There's something else.'

Ahmed turned back.

'I want you to go to The Feathers Hotel. Ask to speak to the manager, and ask him if you may go into the ballroom. When you get there, look at the clock high up on the wall facing the door. There's only one. See if it tells the right time. All right?'

Ahmed frowned.

Angel said, 'That's all?'

'Right, sir.'

‘And before you go, find Ron Gawber and Trevor Crisp and send them in.’

Ahmed closed the door.

A few moments later Gawber arrived.

‘Ah, Ron. It’s time we got down to finding a motive for this murder. Obviously Emlyn Jones is the front-runner, but the super confirms that Jones and his son were at the Potts do at that time. It’s looking certain it couldn’t be either of them.’

‘It must be somebody Pleasant crossed in his business dealings, sir. He wasn’t robbed.’

‘True. He’d eight thousand quid on him. But that jade head is still missing.’

‘But there’s nothing to show that he ever had the thing, is there, sir?’

‘No, there isn’t. There’s only that Gold character who said that he had. If it had been there, I wish I knew where it was now.’

‘SOCO are going through the Pleasant house now, aren’t they?’

‘Yes. I know if it’s there, they’ll turn it up. You’d better check on the phones at Pleasant’s scrapyard and at his house on Creesforth Road. I want to know everybody he phoned over the last two weeks, particularly on that last day of his life, Sunday.’

‘Right, sir.’

Gawber rushed out.

Angel watched the door close then wiped a hand over his mouth. He really began to think that the older he got the more difficult solving cases had become. He really would like to find the motive for Pleasant’s murder. After Bridie had been found butchered and dumped in an oil drum, her sister Jazmin left Emlyn Jones and moved straight in with Charles Pleasant. That would certainly make Emlyn Jones, if he was a normal man, the natural enemy of Pleasant. He couldn’t reach into Jones’s mind and know what he thought, but that would be most men’s feelings. He nodded and then rubbed his chin. However, the photograph of Jones’s presence in The

Feathers with the superintendent apparently showed that he could not possibly have murdered him, and the taker of the photograph, his son, Stanley Jones, was also in the clear. So he must look elsewhere. A thought occurred to him. He reached out for his address book on the table behind him, looked up a number, grabbed up the handset and tapped a number on the telephone pad. He was soon through to the assistant governor of Wakefield Prison.

'The prisoner you have, Larry Longley, Governor, I would like to visit him. He might be able to help me with some inquiries I am making in connection with another case.'

'I'm afraid he won't be any use to you at the moment, Inspector. He is very ill. He is being treated for clinical depression. He won't talk to anybody. Hasn't spoken for the last three months or more. He won't speak to the prison psychiatrist, and in response to simple domestic questions from the officers about his food or clothes he only grunts.'

Angel sighed. He could see another door closing on him.

'In addition,' the assistant governor said, 'I don't think the doctor would permit questions to do with criminal activity. Longley has always maintained his innocence, you know.'

Angel nodded. 'Don't all prisoners do that?'

'Yes, but Longley has declared it, shall we say, with more conviction and persistence than most.'

'He lost both his appeals.'

'I know. I know. You could have a word with the psychiatrist, if you wish. But I am pretty certain you would be wasting your time.'

Angel's jaw muscle tightened, then he said, 'Very well, Governor. Thank you.'

'Sorry I can't be of more help. He might be approachable in a few months.'

'There is something else you could assist us with, Governor. It would be helpful to have a copy of Larry Longley's visiting list.'

Visitors to prisons are limited, carefully vetted and a record kept. Each visitor is required to have a non-transferable pass valid for a specified prisoner on a specified day. Wakefield was particularly exacting in this regard.

'Yes,' he said. 'I can certainly organize that, Inspector. I'll get my secretary to send it in the course of a post or so.'

'Thank you, Governor. Thank you very much,' Angel said and he replaced the handset.

He licked his lips. There was progress … maybe. Sad to learn of the condition of Longley, though. Although the man was a convicted murderer, and sinking into depression, it was tragic to think of him being in a cell twenty-three hours a day for twenty years.

There was a knock at the door.

It was DS Crisp. He was the second Detective Sergeant on Angel's team, a handsome man always turned out in a well-pressed suit and sharp-cut shirt and tie. All the girls liked him and he liked them. Angel frequently spotted him larking about with the prettiest girl in the station, WPC Leisha Baverstock. It happened frequently in the canteen and he had once caught them having more intimate contact momentarily behind the stationery cupboard door in the supplies room.

'You wanted me, sir?' Crisp said chirpily.

'Job for you. There's a man called Stanley Jones. He's not on the PNC but his father is … for drunken driving and indecency. Stanley lives at Flat 14, Council Close, Potts New Estate. He apparently lives with … maybe married to … a woman. I don't have any idea what she looks like or anything else. I want you to find out all you can about her.'

Crisp smiled. This job was something he relished, and would do well, particularly if the woman in question was a good looker.

'Jones works for his father Emlyn at that The Old Curiosity Shop on Old Monk Street,' Angel added.

'I know it, sir. All sorts of weird and wonderful old things, they sell.'

'Aye. I don't know what she does. Anyway, see what you can dig up?'

Crisp grinned.

As he went out, DS Matthew Elliott from the Antiques and Fine Arts squad based in London came in. They had worked together on many a case and were old friends.

'I hope you haven't come on a wild goose chase,' Angel said.

Elliott sighed. 'I've got to follow every lead however slim, Michael. My boss is under great pressure. That jade head is priceless and seems to have inestimable political significance to the people of Xingtunanistan.'

'You'll want me to show you where it was thought to have been hidden then?'

'I thought you'd never ask,' Elliott said, his eyes shining.

It suited Angel to go back to the scrapyard at that time. He had not had the opportunity to spend much time at the scene of the crime. Just being there, often standing around quietly where a crime had been committed, helped him to get the feel of the case and there usually seemed to be something to learn. It was difficult to say what it might be, but all the most successful detectives had said the same thing.

They arrived in the BMW, and Angel pulled it up in the same position as Pleasant had left his Bentley three days earlier. He got out of the car, unlocked the yard gate, opened it by walking with it through 180 degrees then returned to the car door. All the while, he had been glancing across at the site of the road works where the murderer had been waiting. Then something dawned on him. Something that made him stop in his tracks. He asked himself why would the murderer wait there, hiding behind the concrete mixer, while Pleasant, the victim pulled up in the Bentley, got out of the car, unlocked the padlock on the yard gate, walked the gate all the way back, returned to the car, got inside it and then closed the car door before opening fire on him? Pleasant would have made a much easier target when he was actually unlocking the padlock on the gate, pushing the gate open, and when he was returning to the car, than ever he made when he was actually in the driving seat with the door closed. Why would the murderer want to make a smaller target for himself? Had it anything at all to do with him being without shoes? Couldn't see that it had. Couldn't understand why he was without shoes in the first place. This case was full of incongruities. He wondered about the gun. He must have another look at those shell cases. He needed to confirm that they came out of a conventional handgun and not some unusual weapon.

He drove the BMW round to the small office block, moved the forklift, the loose steel plate cover beneath it and unlocked the hidden safe.

Elliott looked on.

Angel lifted open the heavy safe door.

'Ah!' Elliott said, his face brightening. He crouched down and gawped into the empty safe. 'It is certainly big enough, Michael. But if there are no traces—?'

'None,' he said.

Elliott shrugged and continued to stare at the open safe.

Angel looked up and around, suddenly aware that they could be observed. He wondered who could have looked down or across at Charles Pleasant any time when he was opening the safe. It was pretty well sheltered from the world on three sides: the office block, the forklift truck and the perimeter wall. However, he could possibly have been observed by a keen-eyed nosey parker looking from a first floor window in the scruffy lodging house next door. But even if Samson Tickle had ever observed Pleasant's movements, he wouldn't have had a key to the old safe. But there was food for thought.

As Elliott continued to snoop around the safe, Angel meandered out of the scrapyard and up to the rear of the lodging house. The raucous clanging and banging of drums and guitars accompanied by screaming human voices emanating from the electronic speaker in the place assaulted his ears. He pulled a pained face and wondered if it was always like that. He went down the side of the building to the back gate. There was no sign of Tickle, his wife or daughter or anybody else. The gate was open. He went into the small yard and looked around. There was nothing there, just a prop holding up an empty washing line and three wheelie bins for rubbish. He rubbed his chin. The racket was louder and dreadful. He looked upwards. The old stone building seemed eerie and the sky was black as if building for a storm. The din was unbearable. He grunted. There was something wrong. He couldn't put his finger on it, but something was definitely wrong. He was considering whether to knock on the back door when he became aware of another noise. It contrasted wildly and made the racket even more like bedlam. It was his mobile phone ringing. He rushed away from the din, out of the yard, down the step and closed the gate. He answered the mobile as he stepped through the entrance into the scrapyard. It was Ahmed.

'That ballroom clock at The Feathers was spot on correct, sir.'

Angel sighed. 'Right, lad. Thank you.'

'And the super's looking for you, sir. He told me to find you and tell you that he wants to see you, urgently.'

'Right. I'll come straightaway.'

The lines on Angel's forehead creased. Confirmation that the clock was correct meant that Emlyn Jones and his son were definitely in The Feathers at the time of Charles Pleasant's murder. It didn't help much, but it did finally eliminate them. He'd be able to tell Harker that now for a certainty.

He returned to find Elliott still staring at the open safe. He looked up. 'If only this safe could speak,' he said. 'Maybe it could tell us about all the stolen stuff it has held hidden from the world.'

Angel didn't hear him. 'Got to go,' he said. 'The super wants me. You can stay if you want to. I have to go back.'

'No. There's nothing more here for me, Michael. I can't say whether the jade head was here or not,' he said closing the safe door and turning the key. 'Found anything to help you with your case?'

Angel rubbed his chin. 'No. Very strange. Something odd about their back yard,' he said tossing his head in the direction of the lodging house. 'No dog kennel.'

Elliott frowned. 'No dog kennel?'

'Come in,' Harker yelled.

Angel pushed open the door.

'Oh it's you,' Harker continued. It wasn't a welcoming tone. His ginger moustache was twitching. Angel sensed he was in a bad mood.

'Come in. Come in,' he squawked impatiently. He took out his menthol inhaler, removed the cap, stuck it up his nose, sniffed noisily, stuck the top back on and dropped it into his pocket.

'Sit down. Sit down.'

He picked up a pink sheet of A4 from the in tray on his desk and glanced quickly at it. 'Yes. What's this? DS Taylor says you authorized the purchase of 28 pounds of plaster of Paris?'

'That's right, sir.'

'And forty-three plastic boxes? And forty-three padded packets and forty-three first-class, registered express delivery at £6.87 each.'

'It was for a copy of the footprint—'

'I know what it was for,' he bawled. 'The whole thing, including qualified DC's labour, works out at nigh on seven hundred pounds. What do you think SOCO are there for? They are not there to make plaster cast footprints on a production line basis for some new game you've invented.'

Angel's lips tightened back against his teeth. 'That is the footprint of the murderer of Charles Pleasant.'

'So you say.'

'I thought it was a quick, cheap way of informing the national force.'

'And do you think that all the forces in the country are going to line up the villains that pass through their hands in the course of the day, get them to remove their shoes and socks and invite them to put their bare foot on the plaster cast and see if it fits, like they're playing a pantomime game?'

'Well, yes,' Angel said.

'And what about their human rights? Do you not think that their human rights might be infringed?'

'No, sir. If they are villains, they are villains. I wasn't thinking that anyone not suspected of a crime would be asked to check themselves out against the plaster cast.'

'Brussels says that all people, villains or otherwise, are still entitled to be treated and protected in a particular way.'

'They say a lot of things in Brussels, sir,' Angel said.

'You think you can run the force as if it was your own private army.'

'It's not as intrusive as taking fingerprints, sir. For one thing, there are no ink marks on the foot, and—'

'There are strict routines to be gone through – as well you know – before a person's fingerprints can be taken.'

Angel sighed. It was useless arguing. He had run out of sweet reasonableness.

'And the cost comes straight out of my budget,' Harker continued. Then he pulled his full repertoire of facial expressions.

Angel avoided looking at him and said nothing.

'Well, I can't very well stop them now,' Harker concluded.

Angel almost smiled. The plaster casts had been despatched by first-class post yesterday. He would have had a job on!

'Don't do anything like that in future without consulting me, understand?'

'Right sir,' he said and stood up.

'Just a minute. Just a minute,' he said.

Angel concealed a sigh and sat down.

'Did you find anything out about the men who abducted you in the Fat Duck the other day?'

'No, sir. Nothing new there. I've been through the rogue's gallery. They're not in there.'

'What were you doing in a public house at that time of the day, anyway?'

Harker didn't approve of public houses. His face showed it. Angel had seen that same expression on a female prison visitor after she had caught a whiff of Strangeway's gravy.

Angel's knuckles whitened. 'It was my lunchtime. I sometimes meet a snout there.'

Harker rubbed his chin. 'I thought I saw that young DS from the Antiques and Fine Art squad, going into your office?'

'Yes sir. He's looking for a jade head that has been stolen.'

'Oh yes. It's in the Police Review this morning. Don't let him waste your time on that, lad. Let him find it. It's no skin off our nose.'

'Right, sir,' Angel said. He would have agreed to almost anything to get out of Harker's office. There was a lot to do.

CHAPTER 10

He eventually escaped from Harker's office and found Elliott waiting outside his office for him. He looked excited and yet restrained.

'Got a minute, Michael?'

'Of course. Come in. Sit down.'

'I have just heard from my boss in London,' Elliott began. 'The man who held you up, who called himself Gold, was a drug smuggler from Hong Kong whose real name was Abraham Goldstein. Your description fits exactly. He likes to be known as Gold. His two sidekicks were Nelson Shadrack and Seminole Trotter. They originally had a racket stealing expensive cars here in the UK with fake banker's drafts and exporting them with fake documents. They were from Morocco but lately working from an address in Dover.'

Angel looked up, eyebrows raised.

'Have they caught them, then?'

'No.'

Elliott hesitated.

Angel stared at him.

'Got some more info on Goldstein,' Elliott said. His face looked solemn.

'Oh?'

There was an awkward pause.

Angel frowned. 'What?' he said eventually.

Elliott licked his lips. 'It's not very nice. He was found dead in a hotel urinal in Earl's Court,' he said quickly. 'He'd been attacked from behind with a cheese-wire. His head was almost severed.'

Angel wrinkled his nose, turned away momentarily, licked his lips, turned back and said, 'Have they any idea who was responsible?'

'My boss thinks that – from the MO – it will be a Chinese gang member after the reward.'

'And what happened to Nelson Shadrack and Seminole Trotter?'

'Don't know. They seemed to have run off. I expect they've gone to ground.'

'And the jade head?'

He shrugged. 'Nothing.'

Angel sat down.

Elliott said, 'I'll have to go straight back to London, Michael. See what I can find out about Goldstein. You never know, he might have had a lead. There might have been something in his pockets or his hotel room.'

Angel turned to the table behind him. There were two boxes containing plaster footprints of the murderer of Charles Pleasant. He picked up one and gave it to Elliott. 'Here, Matthew, take this. Check this against the right foot of Goldstein. You might find my murderer for me.'

Elliott took it and smiled.

'You might be lucky. Thanks for your help. Goodbye.'

Angel crossed to the door, opened it and shook his hand.

Elliott dashed off.

A split second before he closed the door, he saw a man he thought he knew being accompanied down the corridor by PC John Weightman. He frowned as he returned to his desk. It was somebody in whose company he had been quite recently, and not somebody he had expected to see in the station, but he couldn't put him into context.

He picked up the phone and tapped in a number. Ahmed answered promptly.

'I've just seen John Weightman down the corridor with a man. Find out who he is and what he's doing here.'

As soon as he replaced the phone, he remembered who it was. It was Grant Molloy, manager of Pleasant's scrapyard. He was surprised to find him in the station.

Two minutes later, Ahmed rang back. 'He's one of two men who were fighting in the car park of the Fat Duck, sir. Something to do with a gold chain. His name is Grant Molloy. He's in Interview Room Number One.'

'Where's the other defendant?'

'He's in the security room at reception, sir, with Ted Scrivens.'

Angel replaced the phone and charged up the corridor to reception. He opened the trap in the door of the security room and peered through. Sitting uncomfortably on the fitted bed was a white-whiskered old man in navy blue suit trousers and navy blue suit jacket that didn't match, and a pair of trainers. He was holding a mug of tea and looking up at DC Scrivens who was writing something on a clipboard. On hearing the opening of the trap in the door, the two men turned and looked at it.

'All right, Ted. I'm coming in,' Angel said.

Scrivens straightened up.

Angel let himself in. The security room didn't have a knob or handle on the inside, so he left the door slightly ajar. He looked down at the old man. 'What's going on here?'

Scrivens said, 'This is Fillip Featherstone, sir.'

'Fighting Fillip Featherstone,' the whiskered man said. 'That's why Fillip is spelled with a F. He wouldn't believe me,' he added, pointing to Scrivens.

'He's an ex-boxer, sir,' Scrivens said.

'What's the charge?'

'They were fighting. Mr Featherstone and another man were causing a disturbance in the Fat Duck.'

Angel looked down at Featherstone. 'What were you fighting about?'

'I wasn't meaning any harm. A gold chain except that it weren't gold. He'd tried to pass me a gold-plated chain for a pukka solid 18-carat one. I gave him £100. When I found out it was plated I realized I had been done. I threw it at him. He threw it back and threatened me, so I gave him one. Right in the solar plexus.'

'That's assault, Mr Featherstone,' Scrivens said.

'Well, what would you have done? Let him get away with it?'

Angel pursed his lips. 'And who was this chap? Can you describe him?'

'It's that chap Molloy. The man in the scrap business. He's always hawking stuff around.'

Angel's raised his head. Interesting, he thought. Was there another possible line of inquiry opening up to him? 'Have you bought stuff from him before?'

'Might have.'

'Oh? What sort of stuff?'

He hesitated. 'Gold bits. A muff chain. A woman's charm bracelet. A turquoise ring. Can't think of anything else.'

'And you were satisfied.'

There was more hesitation. 'I suppose so. A mate of mine bought a car battery off of him for ten quid, but it was duff.'

'But you were satisfied with all the stuff he had sold you?'

'Yeah.'

Angel rubbed his chin. 'Where's the chain?'

Featherstone plunged into his pocket and pulled out a gentleman's watch chain. It certainly looked like gold. He passed it over to Angel.

Angel said, 'How do you know it isn't gold?'

Featherstone blinked. 'Huh! There's a little tag soldered on one of the ends near the catch. It has the letters RG embossed on it.'

Angel looked at the end of each catch and eventually found it.

'It stands for rolled gold,' Featherstone said. 'He tried to kid me on it stood for real gold. Huh!'

Angel smiled wryly. He looked across at Scrivens. 'Take this down to SOCO and ask somebody to test this for me and bring it straight back.'

'Make sure you do,' Featherstone called after him.

Scrivens went out leaving the door ajar.

The old man turned to Angel and said, 'Well, are you going to arrest Molloy, then?'

'Are you making a formal charge?'

'Well,' he rubbed his whiskered chin. 'I don't want a fuss. All I want is my hundred quid back. He wouldn't give it to me.'

'There's a matter of a charge against you for disturbing the peace, causing an affray and I don't know what else.'

'You're not serious, are you? What else was I to do?'

Angel frowned. 'We'll see. Wait here.'

Angel went out of the room and closed the door. He went down to Interview Room Number One. There was big PC John Weightman sitting opposite Grant Molloy, who was looking forlorn. As Angel came through, Molloy immediately looked away.

Weightman stood up. 'Do you want to take over, sir?'

'No, John. Not really. What's it all about?'

'Well, sir, I was called to the Fat Duck to find this man with another fighting and shouting in the car park. I stopped the fight and summoned a car to bring them here. This man is—'

'I know who it is, John. Did he say what they were fighting about?'

Molloy turned to look at Angel and spoke out loudly. 'I wasn't fighting,' he said. 'I was only defending myself. I had sold a heavy rolled gold double Albert watch chain to Fillip Featherstone. He was happy enough with the deal at first, then he suddenly changed. He went mad and wanted his money back. He actually threw it at me. I threw it back. Then he came at me like a madman. And that's the truth, the honest gospel truth.'

Angel told him that Featherstone had said that he had been told it was solid gold, but Molloy said that he had told him it was rolled gold from the start and that he would have wanted more than £100 for it if it had been gold. Angel asked him if he was prepared to give Featherstone his money back and Molloy reluctantly agreed, then Angel said, 'Where did you get the double Albert from?'

Molloy looked away briefly, then came back and said, 'It was my father's. I have had it years.'

Angel knew he was lying.

'And was a gold muff chain, a woman's gold charm bracelet and a gold turquoise ring, all your father's also?'

'Yes.'

Angel raised an eyebrow.

Molloy's face went red. 'Well, no,' he said.

'And the car battery you sold for £10 to a friend of Featherstone's, which incidentally, was duff.'

'Well, no,' Molloy said. 'It was stuff mostly brought into the yard by totters, but anybody who was a bit short on their rent, or whatever, would bring stuff in and try and sell it. I've even had three piece suites and televisions offered, usually near Christmas.'

'All the stuff you bought should have gone through Mr Pleasant's books.'

He looked away before replying. 'He was doing all right. You don't run a new Bentley on peanuts.'

'But you bought stuff with his money, didn't give a receipt, didn't enter it in the books, sold it at a profit then replaced the purchase money in the float and kept the difference for yourself?'

'It was only beer money, Mr Angel. Pleasant didn't miss it. I didn't have to buy the stuff in the first place. I wasn't stealing from anybody.'

'It's still dishonest, Molloy.'

'It was the perks of the job.'

'No, Mr Molloy. You are bent.'

'I never took anything from anybody,' he bawled.

Angel turned to Weightman. 'Stay with him,' he said. Then he stood up, went out into the corridor and closed the door. His face was red and his pulse banging in his ears. He didn't like nit picking, penny pinching, conniving little crooks like Grant Molloy, but he was not sure what he could do about it. He stood there rubbing his chin. He could see Charles Pleasant finding out that Molloy had been milking him out of some of the scrapyard profits and perhaps threatening him with the police, and then sacking him. But he couldn't visualize Molloy standing in his bare feet outside the scrapyard gunning Pleasant down in retaliation. The thought of Molloy's bare feet caused him to wrinkle his nose. Besides, Molloy had a key. He could have gunned him down inside the yard. There would have been less risk. He could check his foot against the plaster of Paris model. He charged up the corridor to the CID office. The door was wide open. There were three plain-clothes officers working at computers; the nearest to the door was Ahmed. When he saw Angel he stood up.

'Did you want me, sir?'

'Yes, lad. Look up the PNC and see if there's anything on a Grant Molloy and let me know quickly, then get one of those plaster-cast footprints and take it to Interview Room Number One and leave it with John Weightman.'

'Right, sir.'

He went out of the office and pushed on up the green corridor to his own office. He opened the door and was followed in by Ron Gawber who must have been close behind him. He was waving several pages of close-typed A4.

'Have you a minute, sir? I've got those lists of calls made from Pleasant's home and scrapyard. I've uncovered the identity of all the people called. There doesn't seem to be anything ominous or unexplained.'

Angel turned. 'Really?'

He took the list and glanced down at it. He was particularly interested in calls made on the Sunday Pleasant was murdered. There was none. It was as Gawber had suggested: an inconsequential list of stores, shops and businesses: no friends or family.

The phone rang. It was Ahmed. 'There's nothing about Grant Molloy on PNC computer, sir.'

Angel blinked. 'Right,' he said and replaced the phone.

He told Gawber what Ahmed had said, briefed him on the Molloy and Featherstone situation, instructed him to find the duty JP and get a warrant to search Molloy's house, then he returned alone to Interview Room Number One.

Molloy looked up as Angel walked into the room.

'I can't be kept here much longer. I have my pigeons to feed, you know.'

'You may have to organize somebody to do that job for you, Mr Molloy,' Angel said heavily.

Molloy's face changed and for the first time he looked concerned. He swallowed and wiped the back of a hand across his mouth.

Weightman said, 'Ahmed just brought that box in, sir.'

Angel nodded, picked it up, took off the lid and turned back to Molloy.

'I have here in this box the footprint of the murderer of Charles Pleasant. If your footprint matches it, you'll have more to worry about than your pigeons, I promise you.'

Molloy's eyes opened wide. 'I didn't murder Mr Pleasant,' he protested.

'Well, then you won't mind us checking to see if your foot matches this footprint, will you?'

Molloy's eyes flashed in every direction. He rubbed his mouth. 'I ought to have a solicitor. I know my rights.'

'This is only an informal interview, Mr Molloy. Nothing is being recorded or written down. You've not been charged with anything, yet. We can wait for a solicitor if you insist. But if you didn't shoot Mr Pleasant on Sunday last, you have nothing to fear.'

'I didn't have anything to do with his murder.'

'Take off your right shoe and sock then, please.'

'I've got a warrant to search your house,' Angel said, waving the document under Molloy's nose.

Molloy's mouth opened, then shut. 'You're never satisfied, are you? I told you it wasn't my footprint, but you didn't believe me.'

Angel stood with his hand on the car door and glared into the man's eyes. 'You're bent, Mr Molloy, as bent as old Judge Wimpenny's gammy leg. I don't trust anything you say. Just get in the car and be thankful you're getting a free lift home.'

Molloy muttered something unintelligible as he climbed into the back seat of the BMW. Gawber closed the door behind him and got into the front seat beside Angel.

Angel let in the clutch and the car reversed out of the parking bay then forward through the open gates of the police compound.

'Are my council rates helping to pay for you lumpheads to drive round in luxury like this?'

'Probably,' Angel said. 'And then again, my rates are being used to investigate the disturbance of the peace and whatever other dirty little dishonest tricks you and others like you get up to.'

'There's nothing dishonest about me, I tell you. You'd better be careful what you say, Angel. I could have you up for slander.'

A few minutes later, Angel pulled up outside a terrace house two streets away from Sebastopol Terrace. 'This your house, Mr Molloy?'

'You know it is,' he said, getting out of the car and slamming the door.

'Do you live on your own?'

'Yes,' he said as he pushed the key into the Yale lock on the front door.

As soon as the three men were inside the little house, Angel pointed to Gawber to take the upstairs while he started on the ground floor. The house was clean, tidy and Spartan, so it didn't take long.

Molloy followed Angel through each of the three downstairs rooms, standing in the middle of each room with his hands in his pockets, saying, 'Be careful. If you damage anything, you'll have to pay for it.'

Angel looked systematically through every cupboard and every container, looked behind the pictures and mirrors and then went about testing the floorboards and looking around for loose carpets. He found nothing unusual, incongruous, suspicious or valuable.

Gawber came down the stairs, looked at Angel and shook his head. Angel stood in the hall and rubbed his chin.

Molloy said, 'I told you there was nothing to find. You don't believe anything I say.'

Angel then returned to the small kitchen and looked out of the window. A white painted pigeon loft occupied most of the tiny backyard. He saw a key in the kitchen door, turned it and went outside. The two men followed him, Molloy edging close to his elbow.

There were a dozen or more pigeons cooing and strutting around in the large timber hut, which had a high landing ledge and an opening permitting their easy coming and going. There was wire netting across a large area, and inside the hut were several birds, some on perches, some on open nesting boxes, some feeding from trays suspended from the wall. At the back was a row of twelve closed boxes with holes to enable a bird to shelter. The floor of the wooden building was strewn with a thin layer of clean straw, and at the far end, a door with a big grey padlock on it.

Angel looked at the padlock and then at Molloy.

'Now I don't want you unsettling them and frightening them.'

'Open it up, please, Mr Molloy.'

'It's just my bird loft. There's nothing in there of interest to you, I'm sure.'

'You're probably right,' Angel said. 'But nevertheless, will you open it up, please?'

'This is police harassment,' Molloy said as he unlocked the padlock.

Angel had to take the padlock out of the hasp. He pushed it into Molloy's hand and opened the door. It was big enough for human access.

'If you cause any distress to my birds, I shall make a complaint to your boss.'

Angel stepped up into the loft on to the thin layer of clean, yellow straw. Some pigeons looked at him and chirped mild protests but didn't move from their perches or feeding troughs.

The only places where anything could be concealed seemed to be the row of twelve closed nesting boxes at the back. Those were where Angel immediately approached. He opened them one by one, systematically. There was straw in each. He pulled up his sleeve and reached down below the straw and pulled it up. He searched all twelve boxes. Molloy sniggered each time Angel let the straw fall back in the box. There was nothing.

Angel took one last look round the pigeon loft. Because it was a simple box with a sloping roof, it seemed that there was no place anything could possibly have been hidden. He wrinkled his nose and turned to come out.

Molloy saw his disappointment and grinned. 'There you are. I told you. A complete waste of time.'

As Angel turned, he felt the slightest rocking of a floorboard under the straw; it was accompanied by a tiny squeak. He repeated the movement exactly and the rocking of the floorboard and squeak occurred again. He stopped, frowned, crouched down and rubbed away the straw to reveal the bare floorboards. He looked closely and discovered that a cut with a saw had recently been made. As he cleared more straw, he revealed more new cuts. His breathing became faster. He dived quickly into his pocket and took out his mother-of-pearl-handled penknife.

Molloy and Gawber looked on in silence. Molloy licked his lips while Gawber stared at Angel's busy hands.

Angel opened the knife, slipped the blade in the slits where the cuts had been made and slowly lifted three adjacent pieces of floorboarding, each about two feet long.

Molloy wiped his lips with the back of his hand and said: 'If you find anything under there, I know nothing about it.'

Angel didn't hear him. He pulled away a piece of sacking and saw something shiny and green. With shaking hands, he lifted the object up and placed it on the floor. It caught the bright light and reflected green rays on the yellow straw and Angel's shirt cuffs. He felt his pulse race and his neck and face burn.

It was undoubtedly the missing jade head of Hang Mung Cheng.

Gawber gasped at the sight of it.

Molloy's face went scarlet. His silence indicated that he had become resigned to the inevitable and had given up further thought of pleading ignorance to the existence in his pigeon loft of the remarkable stolen jade artefact.

Angel rummaged down in the cavity to see what else there might be there. He felt something, took out his handkerchief and with it picked up a crudely made key welded to a small spanner. He turned it over and back again to examine it. Meanwhile, Gawber quickly took out an evidence bag from his pocket, unfolded it and held it open to accept the key. Angel nodded and released the key into it.

CHAPTER 11

'That's fantastic, Michael! Absolutely fantastic!' Elliott said on the phone. 'The boss will be delighted. He'll enjoy telling the Empress. She'll be over the moon. She's in hiding in London somewhere, I understand.'

'Good.'

'Has it been damaged at all?'

'It looked fine to me.'

'Good. I can't wait to see it. I expect she'd want to take possession of it as soon as possible. Would that be a problem?'

'No. We have caught the thief. He's admitted it. We have a written statement. The head is secure in the station safe. You can have it as soon as you like. The sooner the better as far as we are concerned.'

'Good,' Elliott said. 'Incidentally, sorry to report, that plaster print didn't come near Goldstein's foot.'

Angel sniffed. Subconsciously he had known it all along, but it could have been a lucky throw.

Elliott sensed his disappointment.

'Sorry, Michael.'

'That's alright.'

'By the by, I discovered that Goldstein was in the employ of the Chief of Police of Xingtunanistan. He's the nephew of the Empress. There was a letter from him and a million Tuong found sewn into the lining of Goldstein's rucksack. That was his fee for the recovery of the head. Worth about eighteen thousand pounds sterling.'

Angel sighed. 'It wasn't enough. It cost him his life.'

Elliott agreed.

'Heard any more about Nelson Shadrack and Seminole Trotter?'

'Not a thing,' Elliott said. 'A warrant has been issued for their arrest and full ID with photographs have been distributed to all ports and airports. I don't expect they'll be seen in the UK again for a while.'

He thanked Angel once more, said that he would be in touch soon and rang off.

Angel replaced the phone, leaned back in the swivel chair and looked up at the ceiling. He went over the events of the past three hours with a warm feeling of satisfaction. After he had lifted the jade head from under the pigeon loft, Molloy had admitted that he had accidentally found Pleasant's old safe and that over weeks of trial and error had contrived a key and opened it; his prints were all over the head and the key so he had little choice but to admit it all. He was just a small-time thief with big ambitions. His footprint didn't fit the plaster cast, so he hadn't murdered Pleasant. That much seemed certain. Angel sighed. What he needed was a good, solid suspect. The favourites had been Emlyn and his son, Stanley, but they had a perfect, apparently indestructible, alibi, so they were in the clear. Surely it couldn't have been Nelson Shadrack or Seminole Trotter in their merciless hunt for the jade head? Goldstein had said that he knew that Pleasant had it hidden in a safe, so it was reasonable to assume that Shadrack and Trotter also knew. He didn't like the idea of those two dangerous lumps rambling round the streets of Bromersley or wherever they had chosen to inhabit. Perhaps when they learned that the jade head had been found and returned to its rightful owner, they'd disappear into the woodwork. He hoped so. This murder inquiry was all highly unsatisfactory. In addition, he had that strange feeling that something wasn't quite right; there was something about the jade head business that still bothered him. He couldn't quite put his finger on it. He wondered if there was something in connection with the finding of the head that he should have attended to. A sort of loose end. He couldn't think what it was. He didn't believe in old wives' tales about inanimate objects having curses on them or anything like that; and the so-called mystery of the Orient was wasted on him. It was no more a mystery than the alleyway between the graveyard of St Mary's Church Bromersley and the back of the Fat Duck most dark Saturday nights. There were places you simply shouldn't be, unless you were with six big men in riot gear each carrying a thumping great baton and a shield. He scratched his head and tried to think. All that he knew was that he would be glad to see the back of that jade head. That thing was a mystery. It was just one of several. There was the dog kennel that wasn't in Tickle's back yard. Where was the damned thing, then? And why were both Emlyn Jones and his son so self-conscious about raw parsnips being found on a cupboard at Emlyn's and on top of women's clothes at his son's, so embarrassing apparently, in each case, that they had to dash to hide them from him. And who shot Charles Pleasant in his bare feet? And why was the murdered man driving his car without shoes?

There was a knock at the door. He looked at it and leaned forward in the chair.

'Yes. Come in.'

It was Ahmed, with a letter. 'Special delivery for you, sir. Looks important.'

Angel blinked.

'Thank you,' he said. He looked at the envelope: it was from the Assistant Governor's Office, Wakefield Prison. It was what he had been waiting for.

Ahmed turned to go out.

'Find Ron Gawber and send him in, lad.'

'Right, sir,' he said and went out.

Angel slit open the envelope, took out the single-page letter and read it. It was very short. He re-read it, and put it down on the desk. He nodded with satisfaction, and rubbed his chin.

Gawber arrived after a minute or two.

'You wanted me, sir?'

'Yes,' he said brightly. 'Come in, Ron. Read that.'

Gawber carefully perused the letter, then he looked up and said, 'In the five years he's been in Wakefield, only four people have been to visit Larry Longley. His son, Abe, frequently – you'd expect that. His solicitor, Alexander Bloomfield, occasionally – he's a necessity. And his sister-in-law – Jazmin Frazer, once on 1 August 2007. That's only last week!'

'Yes. That's a shock to the system.'

'Amazing. You wouldn't expect her visiting him, would you?'

Angel agreed. 'Four days before Pleasant's murder.'

'A week today,' Gawber said pointedly. 'My sister-in-law wouldn't come and see me in prison if I murdered my wife, sir.' Then he added, 'Of course, Larry Longley always claimed he was innocent.'

'Maybe he is. He's appealed twice.'

'But the judiciary have rejected both appeals.'

Angel shrugged. 'Yes.'

Gawber nodded then he said, 'Anyway, sir, we now have the address of Abe Longley. He's moved to Sheffield.'

'Yes. Who can blame him? Trying to start a new life, I suppose. I'll have to see him soon.'

'Do you want me to call on him, sir?'

'No. You know me, Ron. I always like to do the opening inquiries myself.'

Gawber shrugged.

'Tell you what you can do, though,' he said. He turned round to the table behind him and picked up a small box containing four small polythene bags; inside each bag was one of the bullet cases found on the earth next to the footprint at the site of roadworks where the murderer of Charles Pleasant stood. 'Nice run into the country for you. Take those to ballistics at Wetherby. See Professor Wayman. Check on what sort of a gun he thinks fired them. There are the four examples to look at. He might be able to tell us something more than just the calibre.'

'I know, sir,' he said dryly. 'Smile at him and maybe he'll do it while I wait.'

'You got it,' Angel said.

Gawber closed the lid of the box, put it in his pocket and made for the door.

'And if you see Trevor Crisp on your travels, tell him I want to see him,' he called.

'Right, sir.'

The door closed.

Angel sat down. He didn't have time to think of the next priority because the phone rang.

He reached out for it. It was Harker. He started speaking before Angel got the phone to his ear.

'I've just had the Chief Constable on the phone. He wants to know what's happening on the bank robbery front. I told him I'd check up on it and get back to him. So, how far have you got?'

Angel's head came up. He licked his lips. He didn't know what to say. He hadn't done anything at all about it. It was the last question in the world he needed at that time. All his effort had been on the Pleasant murder. 'I'm waiting for SOCO's report, sir,' he said.

'I've just been speaking to Taylor,' he bawled. 'He said that the report was delivered to you yesterday. There were no DNA or prints. Everything's done except for the ballistics on the bullet fired into the bank wall. How far have you got with it?'

'Ah,' he said. 'I have just noticed the report is right here in front of me, sir.'

'Right. Well, how far have you got? Did you find the bogus ambulance?'

'No, sir. Not yet.'

'Well, have you been able to identify anybody on the security tape? The girl was pretty clear in some of those shots.'

'But females can disguise the shape of their faces with cotton-wool and wigs and make-up, sir.'

'I know! I know! I know all that!' he stormed. 'But what can I tell the Chief Constable? He's got the deputy chairman of the Great Northern Bank on his back. He's an old friend of Sir Stanley McPherson, an advisor to the Chancellor of the Exchequer and his brother-in-law is Lord Nile, who is on the Great Northern Bank board. These are very big wheels, Angel. They could make us a lot of trouble. That gang of robbers has to be caught, tried and put away, and we need to be quick about it.'

The names and titles didn't impress Angel at all. If he had included George W. Bush, the Pope and the Cheeky Girls, it would have made the same difference. 'I've really been pulling out all the stops to find the murderer of Charles Pleasant,' he said. 'It's a pretty complicated case, sir.'

'Pleasant?' he roared. 'The scrap dealer?' he roared again. 'Well, you can drop that.'

'It's a murder case, sir,' he protested.

'Yes,' he said, and then he sniffed. 'Let me tell you something that I've discovered in my experience. If a case is complicated, it sometimes pays to leave it a while and let it ripen … let it unravel itself a bit, let the witnesses worry a little, the suspects sweat a little, and the murderer—'

'Go on to murder somebody else,' Angel said, finishing Harker's sentence for him. It was involuntary. He didn't intend to speak out, but it came into his mind and just popped out. He regretted it immediately. He knew it could only make trouble for him.

He heard a sort of intake of breath and then a pause. He knew Harker would be furious; had probably turned purple. Angel had seen him do that when he was really angry. He sat there, hanging on to the phone. He thought about offering an apology, but he didn't think he could manage it. It would stick in his throat.

Eventually, Harker came back. His voice was quivering. Angel could tell he was talking through tight lips. 'You are being ridiculous, stubborn and offensive. I won't forget it. And you still have not given me one thing useful to say to the Chief.'

'Didn't mean to be offensive, sir,' Angel said. He thought very quickly. 'Regarding the robbery, you could say that there were no prints, no DNA, and nothing useful yet from ballistics. However, all personnel have been appropriately briefed to apprehend any suspicious characters, and the machinery for apprehending the bank robbers, as soon as they come out of hiding, is in place.'

'Mmm,' he replied with a sigh. 'That is a right load of waffle, but it might fill the bill. In the meantime, drop that murder case for the time being, and get on to this bank robbery and I don't want any argument about it.'

There was a loud click in Angel's ear and the phone went dead.

Angel blew out a lungful of air and slowly replaced the phone. That was the last thing he wanted to do. He rubbed his mouth and his jaw. He took four deep breaths, stood up, walked round the office, ran his hand through his hair, gazed out of the window for a minute or two seeing absolutely nothing there, returned to his desk, sat down, picked up the phone and tapped out a number.

It was soon answered.

'Ahmed,' he said evenly. 'Find Ted Scrivens and send him in.

'Right, sir.'

'And do you know where DS Crisp is, lad?'

'No sir.'

Angel's lips tightened back against his teeth. 'Well, find him for me. I can never find that lad. I want him urgently, tell him.'

A few minutes later, DC Scrivens, a lanky young policeman who had been on Angel's team for the past four years, knocked on the door and came in.

'Sit down, Ted. And listen up. In reference to that bank robbery on Monday, it involved three men and a woman. You will know that a bogus ambulance was used.'

'Yes, sir.'

'Right, well, according to witnesses, it was a perfect likeness to the real thing, so I suspect that it was a vehicle that had originally been an ambulance, was decommissioned by a hospital, possibly Bromersley, possibly not, bought by the crooks and tarted back up to look like the real thing again. I imagine it was sold to a car auction house either by the hospital or via a specialist dealer who supplies new ambulances and took the old one in on a part-exchange basis. Now, if we could find out how the crooks came by it, or where they had it resprayed and dolled up, and by whom, or where it is hidden now, it might help us to trace the robbers. Got it?'

Scrivens was paying close attention. He nodded. 'Yes, sir.'

'Now, I suggest you start at our local hospital. Find out what they do with their redundant ambulances. Also, you could look up on the PNC for any local vehicle mechanics, panel beaters, body sprayers and so on. Visit them unannounced. Search their premises. Look for signs of a vehicle covered over, or outbuildings that are locked up, or tins of cream paint; that colour isn't used much on private cars these days. Of course, it's perfectly possible that they may have taken off the chrome and the fittings from the old ambulance, sprayed it a different colour and sold it on. However, ambulances have a unique shape. I want you to try and find me a lead. You'll need to use your initiative. I'll leave it with you. Report to me on my mobile anytime if you uncover anything. All right?'

Scrivens face shone. He was pleased to be given the job of making an inquiry under his own steam. It also gave him opportunities to work away from the station office. 'Yes, sir,' he said brightly and rushed off.

Angel watched him through the door and wondered if he had done the right thing. It was really a job for a battle hardened detective sergeant with a snarl; Scrivens was barely a potty trained detective constable with a yelp. But Gawber and Crisp were otherwise engaged. There was nobody else in plain-clothes in his team he could have sent. He consoled himself by reasoning that it would be good experience for him. But where was Crisp? Why didn't he check in? He considered for a moment what he should do next, then he reached out to the phone and tapped in a number. DS Taylor of SOCO answered.

'Ah, Don,' Angel said. 'Are you still at the Pleasants' house?'

'Yes sir. We should be finished tomorrow.'

'Found anything I would want to know about?'

He knew exactly what Angel meant. The list was always the same. He was interested in unusually large quantities of cash or gold, as well as any drugs, weapons, explosives or pornography in any quantity, also anything that seemed to have been stolen.

'No sir. There are files containing share certificates and bonds. I would need an hour or two to make a few phone calls to a stockbroker and the bank to see what they're worth.'

'A rough idea will do, Don. Also I shall want his bank statements. The last twelve month's at least. And his address book.'

'I've seen them. I know where they are, sir. I'll see you get them first thing in the morning.'

'Ta. By the way, what's the house like?'

'Oh,' he grinned. 'Very ornate, sir. Like a proper Mexican Buckingham Palace. Everything of the very best and over the top. The double bed is as big as my front lawn!'

'And how are you getting along with Ms Jazmin Frazer?'

'Oh fine. She sweeps around in a long flowing robe, makes us cups of tea, morning and afternoon. My lads think she's hotter than Nigella.'

Angel didn't even smile. He had noticed the clock. It was half past five. It had been a busy, tiring day.

CHAPTER 12

Steam was escaping through a pan lid on the gas ring, causing it to rattle.

Angel noticed it as he closed and locked the back door.

'Mary,' he called. He turned the gas down as he passed the oven on the way to the fridge.

'Mary!'

She appeared out of the pantry carrying a drum of Saxa.

'Oh. It's you,' she said.

He was taking a beer out of the fridge. He stopped, stared at her and said, 'Who were you expecting, George Clooney?'

She gave him an old-fashioned look. 'Wash your hands and sit down. It'll be ready in ten minutes.'

He poured the beer out into a tumbler, took a sip, removed his coat, loosened his tie and collar, and washed his hands under a running tap. He reached out for a teatowel. Mary headed him off, snatched it away and pushed a hand towel at him.

'Ta,' he said. 'Did I tell you that that scruffy boarding house on Sebastopol Terrace had no dog kennel in its back yard?'

'Yes,' she said. 'Once last night and twice this morning.'

His eyebrows shot up. He sniffed, handed her the towel, picked up the tumbler and strode into the sitting room.

Mary looked at the pan of leeks and turned them up.

After a few moments he came back. 'Any post?'

'The gas bill.'

'Where is it?'

'Somewhere around. I don't know.'

He pulled a mildly annoyed face, muttered something then said, 'I'll find it.'

'I've got something to ask you,' Mary said. 'Been bothering me all day.'

He frowned. He'd had trouble all day at the station. He didn't want any more at home. He stood in the doorway, gripped the tumbler tight, tightened the muscles round his jaw, set his eyes on her and said, 'Aye, what is it?'

'It's been troubling me. I nearly rang the vicar.'

His eyes flashed and stayed open wide. 'The vicar?' he said. 'What is it?'

'I should know, but I can't remember. It's for that competition I'm doing. That quiz.'

He gave a small sigh. His face relaxed. 'Oh that.'

'Don't be so disparaging. It's for £50,000.'

He remembered the gas bill. It would certainly come in handy. He smiled and then took a gulp of the beer.

'Yes,' she said. 'From which mountain top did Moses bring down the tablets of stone on which the commandments were inscribed?'

He looked up, frowned and said, 'Mount Sinai, I think.'

'Mount Sinai! Oh, yes. That's right,' she said as she opened the oven door and peered inside. 'I'll put that in.'

'You'll never win it.'

'You don't know that. Don't be such a wet blanket.'

'Even if you get all the answers right, there'll be hundreds of others you'd have to share with.'

'Not if I'm the only one. Are you going to set the table or not?'

He reached into the kitchen drawer, found the table mats and began picking out knives and forks. 'I've been thinking,' he began tentatively.

She closed the oven door, turned and looked at him.

He licked his lips and said, 'You know how lavender, violets, some roses and perhaps other certain other flowers are used to give off a pleasant, fresh smell around clothes, bedding, people and so on?'

'Yes?' she said giving him a strange look. She was wondering where the question was leading to.

'Well, do parsnips have any special quality other than being a vegetable for eating? I mean, might someone have good reason to put them among clothes or in a potpourri, or in a vinaigrette or in a cupboard, for some misguided, maybe, or perhaps little-known, reason?'

She shook her head patiently. 'Not that I know of, Michael. And you've asked me that before. Several times, actually, in the past two days.'

'Have I? Sorry, love.'

'Now look here,' she said determinedly. 'That's work and it's six o'clock almost and you're home now. Forget about parsnips. There's plenty of time tomorrow to worry about them.'

He blinked. He knew she was right. She was absolutely correct in what she had said.

'Yes, love,' he said. He resolved immediately to stop tiring himself out needlessly. He wasn't even going to think about work. He was going to have dinner, a few beers and watch television. He thought it was the night for *Bad Girls*.

Mary turned back to the oven.

He nodded, then ambled into the sitting room.

Two minutes later, Mary called, 'It's ready, Michael! I'm serving it out.'

But he didn't hear her call. He was concentrating on a piece of paper he was holding. He had found the gas bill and with a stub of a pencil from his pocket he had drawn something on the back of it. He was turning it round to observe it from different positions. The drawing looked remarkably like the outline of a cream-coloured root vegetable.

'Michael!' she bellowed.

He hurriedly stuffed the paper into his pocket.

'Good morning, sir.'

'Come in, Ron.'

'I saw Professor Wayman, sir. He didn't think there was anything at all fishy with the shells. He confirmed that they were fired from the same gun, and that it was a .32 calibre and probably a Walther PPK/S. That's all he could say.'

Angel rubbed his chin. 'So there was nothing peculiar about the gun.'

'He was pretty confident about it, sir.'

'Right. That makes the way Pleasant was shot straightforward. Nothing else about this case can be said to be that. Are you expecting to go out this morning?'

'No sir. I've a lot of paperwork to catch up on.'

'I might have got a job for you.'

'I'll check with you if anything crops up, sir.'

'Right.'

The door closed.

The phone rang. It was Taylor.

'About those shares and bonds from Pleasant's files at home, sir.'

'Yes, Don?'

'The shares certificates were for old issues of good shares that had had their names changed for some reason and were now valueless. New certificates to replace them would have been issued at the time; the old ones are now just so much paper. Pleasant's stockbroker said that he had sold all his holdings over the years.'

'Really?' he said, frowning.

'Similarly, the bonds had all been cashed, sir. The banks and building societies didn't actually call for the actual bond certificates to pay out on redemption. The owner's signature, clearing bank branch address and account number is enough for them to pay out.'

'That'll be a shock to Jazmin Frazer.'

'There's something else, sir. On checking through Pleasant's bank statements, sir, seems to me there's a regular debit order of £800 a week being paid out to an account simply called Hellman.'

Angel looked up, eyebrows raised. 'Oh? And who or what is Hellman?'

'No idea, sir. Thought you might like to know straightaway.'

He nodded. It could be a perfectly legitimate payment for something, repayment of a loan, hire purchase or even rent. Or it could be blackmail money.

'There's no attempt at concealment, Don?'

'No, sir.'

'When did the payments start?'

'The cheques are itemized on all the statements I've got and they go back a year.'

'Right, lad. Sounds innocent enough, but find out what Hellman is and what the money is for and get back to me.'

'Right, sir.'

He replaced the phone.

He scratched his chin. Hellman? Who the hell was Hellman?

Then he remembered that he had been about to make a phone call before Gawber had interrupted him. It would have been to send Ahmed up to SOCOs for the Great Northern Bank's security tapes. But now he was considering that that also could wait.

There was something niggling him about Emlyn Jones and his son. They were a couple of prime criminals, and Angel was as passionate about criminals, as chocoholics were about chocolate. Ever since Stanley Jones had shown him that photograph of Harker and Emlyn Jones, taken by himself in the ballroom at 4.30 on that Sunday afternoon, Angel had been suspicious. Something had been bothering him. Something impossible to describe, but he knew that they were, or had been, up to no good, and he intended finding out what it was. He knew that Emlyn Jones and his son were concealing something, and it was much, much more than mere parsnips.

He decided he would make some feathers fly. It was the only way. He reached out for the phone and sent for Gawber.

'I want you to go on a bit of old-fashioned following. Are you up for it?'

His face brightened. 'Of course, sir.'

'Has your car a full tank of petrol? You might need it.'

'No, sir.'

'Push off, get it filled up and get your car checked off and meet me back here ASAP.'

Gawber grinned and rushed out. The door closed.

Angel rubbed his chin.

Angel walked through the open doorway of The Old Curiosity Shop. It wasn't yet busy. There were no customers. Two young ladies in smart blue dresses were standing behind glass display counters at opposite sides of the shop. They were doing nothing in particular and trying not to look bored. They watched Angel approach a small Victorian table which converted into a sewing basket; next to it was a doll which had a pincushion for a stomach with twenty or thirty eight-inch, ten-inch and twelve-inch long hat pins with various pearl, Whitby jet or pretty coloured glass ends sticking out of it.

Suddenly, from behind a large bookcase, a shiny young man in a shiny blue suit appeared and made a beeline for him. It was Stanley Jones. His black hair was oiled down and shone in the bright white shop lights, and his chin was jutting out. He had an angry look about him. His eyes stood out like bilberries on stalks. He came right up close to Angel and whispered in his ear.

'You shouldn't come in here. Not in shopping hours. Not when customers are around. It'll give the shop a bad name.'

Angel pulled away from the hot breath and said, 'But you have no customers, Mr Jones. The shop is empty; haven't you noticed?'

He moved further into the shop, passing a gathering of teddy bears of various prices, ages and conditions. Stanley

Jones followed close behind, all the while becoming more agitated.

Angel stopped at a shelf of large interesting glass vases, gold fish bowls and colourful antique chamber pots all filled with water. Each also had a red rubber ball in the water; some of the balls were floating, some were sunk and some were in between.

He hovered there a few moments.

Stanley Jones edged closely up to him again. 'What do you want,' he said breathily, then looked round at the two shop assistants to see if they had heard him.

One was yawning, the other about to yawn.

'What is the purpose of the balls in the water,' Angel asked mischievously.

The young man stuck out his chin belligerently. 'To check that the vessels are sound, of course,' he snarled.

At that moment, Angel heard the little door to the tiny office under the stairs behind them close, and the unmistakable fruity loud Welsh voice said, 'We couldn't sell a leaking Victorian chamber pot to a wealthy American, Inspector Angel, now could we?'

Angel turned round. Emlyn Jones was standing there in a shiny black velvet suit, smiling as always, with his hand on the door knob. Jones waved a gently dismissive hand at Stanley who glared at Angel, before turning away and slowly walking to the other end of the shop to disappear round the back of a bookcase of old leather-bound books.

'Youth is so beautiful, Inspector, don't you think?' Jones said. 'So much future ahead of them. So much time to achieve whatever they want. Yet they are always in a hurry. You see them running hither and thither without a moment to lose, pushing past you on the pavement, in the shops, overtaking in a car, but you never see them arrive anywhere, do you?'

'No,' Angel said politely.

He looked at the man, pursed his lips and wondered what he was really thinking. What secret was behind that oily smile. After twenty-one years of marriage, Charles Pleasant had taken Jones's wife from him only four short years earlier, providing the man with a most powerful motive. But Jones had the most perfect alibi, the absolutely indisputable alibi, in wonderful photographic colour. So had his son, Stanley, who also had a motive. Stanley had taken that crucial photograph. So his alibi was sound. They positively had both been there. In the ballroom. At 4.30. Harker had confirmed it. Superintendent Harker had positively confirmed it.

Angel rubbed his chin.

Jones said, 'Now then, did you want to see me about something particular, Inspector? Would you like to come into my office? It is private and very quiet in there.'

He opened the door of the little cubbyhole under the stairs.

Angel nodded and went inside. Jones sat behind the little desk and Angel sat opposite him.

'Isn't this cosy?' Jones said with a grunt of a laugh. 'It is almost coffee time. Or would you like something a little stronger?'

'Nothing for me, thank you,' Angel said.

'No? Well, what is it I can do for you, Inspector?'

'Well, I'll tell you, Mr Jones. It's like this. You know my business. I have a murder to solve. Perhaps you can help me.'

'I don't know why you've come to me, Inspector. But I'll try. Always willing to help the law in any way I can. You know that.'

'It's a little complicated, Mr Jones, but I'll try to keep it simple. There is a man, you see … a married man … been married twenty-one years. To a beautiful woman, and they had a son. Now four years ago, his wife left him to go to live with another man, a very rich man.'

Jones's eyebrows shot up. He dropped the smile and rubbed a hand across his mouth. 'You're getting very close to home, Inspector,' he said quietly. 'Where are you going with this … this story?'

'The rich man is murdered and the first thing the ex-husband does is have his son present a photograph to me, taken by him, of his father sitting with a senior police officer with a clock showing the crucial time. The photograph … you might say … is the pictorial representation of the absolutely perfect alibi.'

'Yes. Well what's wrong with that? It must make your life simple in one way, Inspector. It makes for eliminations, doesn't it? The photograph obviously and simply means that we … my son and I … could not have murdered Charles Pleasant.'

'It does. But it means more than that, Mr Jones. Much more. It means that you knew the day and the time the murder was planned to take place.'

'No. No. I see how it may look, now. But it's obviously a coincidence. It's a coincidence, pure and simple.'

'There was nothing pure and simple about it, Mr Jones. You and your son Stanley are accessories before the fact. As more evidence comes out, it is possible that you will be charged and, if found guilty, you could be awarded a custodial sentence.'

Jones's face changed. 'What? Aaaah! Not again! *I couldn't stand it*!' he shrieked uncontrollably. Then his eyes slid slyly in Angel's direction to see how he had reacted to the telltale outburst.

Angel had missed nothing. 'I know all about that business in your car with that … girl,' he said.

Jones's eyes flashed. 'She told me she was 18, I swear it.'

Angel acknowledged the reply with a non-committal wave of a hand.

Jones played with his bottom lip, nipping it gently as his mind assimilated all that was happening around him. After a few seconds, the smile returned and, slapping the flat of his hand on the top of the desk, he said: 'This is ridiculous! You would have to prove it first, Inspector, and you could never do that because it simply isn't true. It's a coincidence, that's what it is. A pure coincidence. Any right thinking, God-fearing jury would see that.'

'I would not put money on it, Mr Jones. If I uncover any evidence to show that you were involved in the murder of Charles Pleasant in any way at all, any God-fearing jury would inevitably believe that there would simply be too many coincidences for you not to be involved in the murder!'

The Welshman's eyes flashed again. 'That would be very unjust. It cannot be true. No. No. No. God knows I am as innocent as a newborn babe. I must go to the chapel and light a candle. Six candles. My life is an open book. A dedication to the Ten Commandments, which I reiterate daily and endeavour to keep. I made a little mistake in the past, but I was tempted. Tempted by a serpent … in a skirt. You should read the psychiatrist's report on the woman. It was in no way my fault.'

Angel didn't believe a word he said. Jones might just as well have been talking to a tin of corned beef. After a calculated pause, he leaned forward in a confidential manner and quietly said, 'Of course, there may be a way … this unpleasantness could be … minimized.'

Jones's eyes opened wide for second, then he leaned forward. 'Minimized?'

'Very simply,' Angel said with a nod.

Jones leaned even nearer. 'Simply? How?'

'Simply tell me who murdered Charles Pleasant.'

Jones jumped back. 'I have no idea,' he bawled. 'Absolutely no idea. On my sainted mother's grave, I tell you Inspector Angel, I have not the slightest notion. Fancy you thinking I knew anything about that.'

Angel was satisfied with the interview. It had proceeded pretty well as he had expected.

He took his leave of a worried and irritated Jones, came out of The Old Curiosity Shop, walked round the corner out of the possible sight of the shop windows, took out his mobile and tapped in a number. It was promptly answered.

'I've just come out of the shop, Ron. He should be leaving any minute now.'

'Right, sir.'

CHAPTER 13

Angel returned to the office and shuffled through the pile of envelopes on his desk looking for SOCO's report on the Great Northern Bank premises. He found it. He was relieved to find that it was only five A4 pages. It was only five pages because, as usual, in the cases that came his way these days, there was so little forensic. If the crime scene had been crowded with fingerprints, footprints and DNA it would have been a much easier job catching the robbers. Criminals were becoming more sophisticated every day, catching up with modern scientific advances. However there were the security tapes. He reached out for the phone. He was about to tap in Ahmed's number when there was a knock at the door. It was Crisp. He came in all smiles. He was carrying a stone-coloured paper folder.

Angel's lips tightened. He banged down the phone. 'Where the hell have you been? I've had Ahmed trying to reach you for two days. Why didn't you report in? Is your mobile on the blink again?'

Crisp looked stunned. 'What's the matter, sir?' he said.

'You know damned well what's the matter. I give you a job. Tell you to keep in touch, and you disappear into outer space. When anybody tries to contact you, you're unreachable.'

'I have been hard at it, sir, honest. And look, I'm here now.'

'About time. What is the matter with your mobile?'

'Nothing, sir. It's been switched on most of the time.'

He pointed to the chair, directing Crisp to sit down.

Angel couldn't sustain a verbal offensive against him. He was far too intelligent to be in any way worried about anything Angel might say. If Angel really wanted to frighten him, he'd have to formally discipline him in writing, which might affect his promotion and pay. He didn't want to go that far, but Crisp really tried his patience.

'Well, I hope it's all been worthwhile. What have you got?'

Crisp opened the paper file. 'Her name is Chantelle Moses, sir. She is 29, a bit older than Stanley Jones. She has a record. Shoplifting and soliciting when she was a teenager. Nothing recently. Mother not known. Father in Armley, half way through a sentence of four years for stealing two hundred and forty metres of copper signalling wire near Doncaster, off the main Aberdeen to Kings Cross track in 2005.'

He held out a computer print of a photograph. Angel took it.

'That's Chantelle ten years ago.'

Angel looked at the print. It was head and shoulders of a young woman with frizzy black hair. She was probably pleasant looking, but it was a prison photograph and she seemed to be looking at the photographer defiantly. He read the description in small print underneath. Height 5' 4". Weight 6 st 9 lb. Black hair. Brown eyes. Small brown mole on left temple. Date of birth 12 April 1978 (Cardiff Royal Free Hospital). Father: Jake Moses (West Indies). Mother: Maria Thomasina (Ireland).

'What's she doing now?'

'I think she's just playing house for Stanley Jones, sir. During the two days I was watching her, she only went out to the shops. That's all she did all day.'

'You didn't approach her, then?'

'No, sir.'

'Didn't fancy her?' Angel jibed.

Crisp had a reputation for chasing anything in a skirt.

He knew Angel was teasing him. He shrugged in a non-committal way.

'Anything else?' Angel said.

Crisp produced six more photographs. 'I took those yesterday.'

The photographs were of a very smart young woman: black hair brushed straight and combed back, and dressed in blouse, a short skirt and high boots and carrying a shoulder bag. The photographs were of her locking the door of the flat and coming out of various shops carrying bags or boxes of shopping.

Angel looked at the photographs carefully. He blinked and said, 'Big difference. She's wearing more make-up than the cast of Showboat. Are you sure these are of the same woman? Prison photographs are like those on a passport.'

'Oh yes, sir. Chantelle Moses.'

Angel then rubbed his chin.

'You're sure? Did you see the mole on her left temple?'

Crisp's mouth opened. He said nothing. It closed. Eventually he said, 'No, sir.'

'Did she spot you, do you think?'

He grinned confidently. 'No, sir. Not a chance.'

'There doesn't seem to be any food in her shopping. Did she only go into dress shops?'

Crisp frowned. 'No sir. She went into a shoe shop, several shoe shops, in fact. And a jeweller's.'

Angel's eyebrows went up. 'A jeweller's?'

'But mostly dress shops.'

Angel rubbed his chin. 'Right!' he suddenly snapped. 'Get back to her. Stick to her.'

Crisp's face dropped. He couldn't believe what he'd heard. He hesitated then said, 'You're not wanting me to hang around this tart all day just to get a charge of soliciting, are you, sir?'

‘No. There’s much more to it than that, lad. Didn’t you think she was spending rather too much? And on what you and I might call luxury items? Do you think Emlyn Jones would pay his son enough money to enable his live in girlfriend to spend all her time shopping? No. There might be something fishy there. Where’s she getting the money? Is she back on the game? See where she goes, what she does. And for goodness sake, don’t take silly risks, but see if you can check out that mole. Make sure you’ve got the right suspect.’

Crisp stood up.

‘And give Ahmed your mobile number,’ Angel said. ‘And ring in at least once a day.’

‘Right, sir,’ Crisp said in a loud, firm voice.

Angel was almost convinced that he would, as the door closed. But not altogether.

Although the murder investigation could hardly be said to be going well, Angel had all his team out on inquiries, and felt that he ought to allocate some of his time to investigating the robbery of the Great Northern Bank. He felt it was necessary because he never knew when the honey monster might appear and ask for another report on progress and he didn’t want to face that awkwardness again. He didn’t agree with Harker’s order of priorities. In his view, the solving of a murder case must always rank as more important than any bank robbery, however well the Chief Constable knew the deputy chairman of the bank!

He quickly shuffled through the envelopes on his desk to find SOCO’s report; he found it, skimmed through it again and brought himself up to speed. He was at the stage of needing to see the CCTV tapes, so he got Ahmed to collect them down from SOCO, copy them and transfer them to a disc, then the two of them viewed them in his office on his laptop.

The beginning of the playback had a caption that read: ‘Front Door’. It was outside the bank showing the arrival of the woman who had pretended to be pregnant. He slowed the playback. She was in a long shot so not very much was revealed except that she had a lot of hair, that it was black or dark brown and that she was wearing a wedding ring. She disappeared inside the bank. He ran the recording on at high speed. Soon the phoney ambulance arrived with the two phoney ambulance men. He stopped the tape and zoomed on to the rear of it.

'Ahmed,' Angel said. 'Make a note of that index number. And check it out. I don't suppose it will get us anywhere.'

'Right, sir.'

Then Angel clicked on the fast forward until the playback showed the two men carrying the woman out on a stretcher. There was nothing distinctive about the men except that they both were young and had beards and moustaches. They slid the stretcher and the woman into the back of the ambulance and accordingly sped away out of the range of the camera. There was nothing of interest on the rest of that tape, so he ran the playback up to the 'Rear Door' caption. It simply showed the ambulance arrive and reverse up to the rear of the bank; a woman in a plain dark trouser suit, who looked similar to the woman who had worn much more feminine clothes earlier and played at being pregnant, jumped out of the cab, opened one of the rear doors, then climbed back into the driving seat. Angel noticed that she was not wearing any finger rings. Almost immediately the back door of the bank opened. The two robbers wearing overalls and masks emerged, they threw the bags into the back of the ambulance, jumped in and pulled the door to from the inside as it drove swiftly away. The next caption read: 'Security Door'. There were many more close-up shots of the gang's faces. The woman's abundant and curly black hair covered most of her ears, down her forehead, and over part of her cheeks; it was so profuse that Angel concluded that it must have been a wig, worn by a woman determined not to be identified from a CCTV recording. By making comparisons with the height of the door, he estimated that she was about 5' 4" in height. The two male robbers were clearly wearing false beards and moustaches throughout, also masks when they were in the secure area. He ran the playback to the end then concluded that, even though the bank's CCTV cameras had been well placed, and were in colour and in focus, he had not learned very much from them. The raid had clearly been organized and carried out in a most professional way. The solving of this crime was not going to be easy. The gang leader had been most meticulous; even the female member of the gang had removed her wedding ring when she changed her role from pregnant young wife to ambulance driver.

He began to close down the laptop, turned to Ahmed and said, 'Thank you. Check that ambulance number. See where it leads to. And let me know.'

'Right, sir,' Ahmed said and went out.

As soon as the door closed, Angel sighed and wrinkled his nose. He was not a happy man. He was plagued with questions. He had been solving crimes now for nearly sixteen years but he had never had two cases so full of annoying, even ridiculous issues. For instance, why would a man commit murder with no shoes on? What sort of idiot walks about with no shoes on, waving a gun around? What's the reason? And why had the victim no shoes? Two men without shoes? Both the murderer and the victim were walking about without shoes. It didn't make any sense.

He ran his hand through his hair.

And why are the Joneses so secretive about having parsnips in the house? What's so special about parsnips, for goodness sake? Were they used in connection with the murder of Charles Pleasant? There must be something dishonest about them. And he didn't trust Emlyn Jones. He was sure he had something to do with Pleasant's murder. But what? You can't poison anybody with them. You can't shoot them or knock anybody unconscious with them. They are not even slippery like a banana skin. You couldn't put one on the top of the cellar steps to get rid of a rich, elderly relative with any certainty; he'd likely catch it with his stick without noticing and send it rolling down the stairs.

'What possible use is a parsnip other than to eat the damned thing?' he called out loud in exasperation.

And how did that woman manage to flood the bank ten minutes after she'd left the place? The plumber said it was something to do with the ballcock, but he couldn't quite see what. Neither did he know how she had managed to delay the leak for ten minutes to allow her and the phoney ambulance to make a clean getaway.

And why is it that at the boarding house next door to the scrapyard they say they have a dog and a dog kennel, but the dog kennel is nowhere to be seen?

The phone rang. He reached out for it. 'Angel.'

It was Don Taylor. 'Excuse me, sir, but I've found out what that standing order for £800 a week payable to Hellman is for, sir.'

'Oh yes, what?'

'Well it's to a Mr Hellman. He owns The Hacienda. Pleasant was paying him £800 a week rent.'

Angel's eyes narrowed. 'The Hacienda? £800? Pleasant doesn't own it then? Sounds a lot, £800 a week?'

'Well, you know the price of houses today, sir. I've spoken to Mr Hellman. He bought the house from Pleasant in 2003.'

Angel took the news in only slowly. 'Who is this Hellman, then?'

'He's a local wholesale butcher … in a biggish way. Has premises on St George's Road. A couple of retail shops. A stand in the market. Sells pre-packed meat lines like potted meat, salami and sandwiches to local factory canteens and so on. Imports and sells corned beef, tongue and other tinned meats. Well respected. He sounds kosher, sir.'

Angel blinked. 'You seem to know a lot about him?'

'I knew you'd ask, sir.'

Angel nodded and smiled. He replaced the phone. He rubbed his chin. He was amazed to learn that the house didn't belong to Pleasant. He wondered about it briefly. Over the past twelve years, the Frazer sisters, between them, had certainly made a good job of spending his money.

The phone rang. He reached out for it. It was Gawber.

'Yes?' Angel said.

'I followed Emlyn Jones to the block of flats in Sheffield where Abe Longley lives, sir. I couldn't follow him in, of course. I'm waiting outside.'

Angel nodded. He had thought that Jones might contact his nephew, Abe, and warn him that he might be approached by the police and to be guarded about what he might say. But he was surprised that Jones would drive the fifteen miles to Sheffield, presumably to avoid creating the record of a phone call and the possibility of being overheard.

'Right, Ron. Well, hang on there and see where Jones goes next. Follow him and ring me on my mobile. I'll get over there just as soon as I can. See what Abe Longley has to say for himself. All right?'

Gawber rang off.

Angel glanced across the desk. It was very untidy. Papers all over the place. Correspondence read but not dealt with. Messages on backs of envelopes. Mysterious words scrawled on sticky notes. Not his usual style, but he decided that there was nothing he couldn't leave until later. His blood was up. He was determined to get to the bottom of the case. He hoped that following Jones's urgent visit to Abe Longley he might trip across some vital clue or titbit of information that would be the key to solving this case. Jones was very careful. Very careful indeed. And extremely clever. His attention to detail was quite exceptional. If he was up to anything criminal, Angel knew he'd need to draw on all his skills to catch him out.

He dashed out of the office and down the corridor.

CHAPTER 14

He arrived outside a group of four concrete blocks of high-rise flats on the north side of Sheffield. He found the block where Abe Longley lived and drove the BMW round looking for Gawber's car. He couldn't see it so he assumed Jones had gone and that he would be following him. He parked the BMW at the foot of the block, among another twenty cars or more. He made his way towards the lift doors. Rude words and hieroglyphics were spray-painted on them. He decided to walk up the steps to the first level, so changed direction. Four small girls were playing a jumping game on the steps. As he approached, a fat woman appeared from nowhere. She picked up the smallest girl, put her under arm, shouted something at the other three and rapidly shepherded them behind the steps along a corridor into the bowels of the building.

He made his way up to the first floor and along the outside walkway, found the flat he wanted and knocked on the door. He had to wait what seemed for ages before the door was opened. A man answered it. He opened it about fifteen inches and held it in position with his foot while he buttoned up his shirt and tucked it into his trousers.

'I'm Detective Inspector Angel. I'm looking for Mr Abe Longley?'

'That's me.'

'I'm making inquiries about the murder of Charles Pleasant.'

'Oh yes,' he said, showing no emotion or surprise. Then he hesitated and looked sideways behind the door. He looked uneasy.

Angel sensed that there was something or somebody behind the door. His heart began to hammer in his chest.

'I need to come in,' he said. 'There are some questions I want to put to you.'

Longley looked back at him. He licked his lips. 'It's not convenient just now. Can you come back later?' he said. He gave another glance behind the door.

Angel's fists tightened. 'No,' Angel said. 'I've come all the way from Bromersley and—'

He broke off, grabbed the edge of the door and gave it a mighty push, sending Longley backwards toward a sideboard behind him. There was a thud and the rattle of china and drawer handles. Angel peered behind the door and saw a girl with long stringy hair, big frightened eyes and wearing a smart white astrakhan coat. She was waiting behind the door. When she saw him, she screamed and put her fingers to her mouth.

Longley recovered himself and came up to Angel with his fists clenched.

The girl screamed again, then she ran across the room bare foot and out through the door at the other side of the flat.

Longley's face was red and his jaw muscles tight. 'You didn't have to do that,' he said. 'You've frightened her.'

'I'm sorry. I thought you had somebody threatening you. I find that people hiding behind doors aren't usually very friendly.'

Longley looked at him for a moment, then slowly lowered his fists.

Angel closed the door and looked round the little room. The table, sofa and floor were littered with store bags, boxes and loose tissue paper. 'Your wife been on a shopping spree?'

Longley looked away and ran his hand across his mouth. 'Yeah, well, I suppose you could say that. She's not my wife. She doesn't live here. Her name's Penny Furnace; she's a neighbour.' He suddenly spotted something amid the wrapping paper and reached down for it.

Angel saw it: it was black, small and frilly.

Then Longley saw a stocking on a chair, and another on the table. He snatched at them and squeezed them in his hands to make them small.

He went to the room door. A hand attached to a slim bare arm reached into the room. He pushed the stuff silently into it. The hand and arm disappeared and then came out again. He frowned and looked round the room and then at the floor. He found one shoe and then another. He put them into the girl's hand. The hand and arm were pulled in and he closed the door. He returned, avoided looking directly at Angel, blew out an impatient measure of air and said, 'Yeah, well, what do you want from me? Anyway, what happened to that bastard, Minto?'

'Detective Inspector Minto? He retired,' Angel said. 'May I sit down?'

Longley moved some wrapping off the sofa and banged it on to the table. 'Right bastard he was.'

Angel sat down. He guessed that Minto was the officer who had brought the case against his father four years earlier, that had resulted in Larry Longley being sent to prison for life. He could well understand Abe Longley's resentment, but he really didn't want to dwell on any history.

'You said something about Charles Pleasant,' Abe Longley said. 'You're making inquiries about his murder? Well, I've just had my uncle here. He told me you would be coming. He warned me to be careful. I don't know what for. I've got nothing to be careful about. Huh! My mother's been murdered and my father's wasting away in jail; what have I got to be careful about? As long as I'm not set up for murdering Pleasant like my Dad was set up for murdering my mother, I should think I'm all right.'

'You understand, Mr Longley, I have to follow up all persons who have a motive for killing him. And you wouldn't deny you have a motive?'

'He murdered my mother and got my father in prison for it; I'll say I've a motive. I wouldn't deny it at all. I'm glad he's dead. I hope he rots in hell, but I didn't kill him.'

Angel didn't react. He understood the man's feelings.

'So I simply need an alibi. I need to know where you were between four and five o'clock last Sunday afternoon?'

'That's easy. I was here with Penny all afternoon.'

Angel nodded and pursed his lips.

Longley turned his head and shouted: 'Hey. Penny. Are you there?'

There was a squeak of hinges and the room door opened, but she didn't make an appearance.

'Come on in, Penny.'

First one eye, a nose and half a face, and then the other half of Penny appeared. She was dressed in a white overall dress with the words 'Moo Moo Ice Cream' embroidered in red on the lapels. She wore a pretty pendant necklace of rubies and pearls and two or three rings on every finger except the third on her left hand. She stared at Angel as if she was expecting him to jump out and attack her as she moved sideways round the room with her back to the wall.

'This is Inspector Angel. He's a policeman.'

Angel smiled at her. She smiled back briefly with her mouth, but her big eyes were weighing up the man and the situation.

Longley said: 'He's come about the man who murdered my mother. I told you about it.'

'Oh yes,' she said. 'Pleased to meet you, Inspector, but if you'll excuse me, I've got to go to work. I'm going to be late.'

'The inspector wants to know where I was on Sunday afternoon. Will you tell him?'

'He was with me, here, Inspector. Watching a video, some of the time. Then my mother and father came in for a cup of tea.'

'What time was that?'

'Half past four,' she said. 'Look at the time, Abe. I'll have to go.'

'Half past four?' Angel said.

'Yes,' she said.

'Are you sure?'

'Positive,' she said, then she made for the door, stopped, glanced at Angel, came back, put her arms round Longley's neck, gave him a big, hard kiss, whispered something that sounded like, 'Thank you. See you tonight.' Then she made for the door.

'I'll need your full name and address,' Angel called but the door had closed and she was gone.

Longley turned to look at Angel with his mouth open.

Angel thought Longley was surprised and embarrassed at the young woman's show of affection.

'I'll need her name and address, and her mother and father's name and addresses.'

'Her name is Penelope Furnace and her parents are Ken and Barbara Furnace. They all live two doors away at number 114.'

'I'll have to speak to them.'

'Of course. Why not?'

'Are you in full-time employment at the moment, Mr Longley?'

He sniffed. 'I am not doing a lot at the moment. I had a job preparing meat for a supermarket, but it merged with another supermarket and powers that be decided to do the prepping at their HQ so I was surplus to requirements. I could have taken a job at nights doing a different job at less money, but I didn't want to.'

'So you're presently unemployed?'

'Well, yes. But I'm looking round.'

'Have you any qualifications?'

'Nothing formal. Spent all my working life in the meat trade.'

'Taking after your father? There should be plenty of opportunities in and around Sheffield for an experienced butcher.'

'Yes. Might even get my own shop,' Longley said.

Angel smiled politely and rose to his feet. 'That's all for now. I must call on Mr and Mrs Furnace.'

Longley nodded and opened the door for him. 'Turn right and it's two doors along. A hundred and fourteen.'

'Thanks very much. Good luck with the job hunting.'

He sauntered along the walkway up to the door of flat number 114, two doors away. A genteel lady in her fifties answered the door. It was Mrs Furnace, mother of Penelope. She welcomed him and invited him into the flat. She introduced him to her husband. It seemed that they were watching a DVD on a large new slimline television set. It was the only bright piece of furniture in the dreary sitting room.

The Furnaces seemed to have taken Abe Longley into the bosom of their family and were happy to confirm that they had certainly taken tea with their daughter, Penelope at Abe Longley's last Sunday at 4.30 p.m.

Angel returned to Bromersley well satisfied with his afternoon's work thus far. He was travelling along Sheffield Road, checked the time on the BMW dashboard clock and saw that it was just short of four. If he was quick, he thought, he could call on Jazmin Frazer and clear up some points that had been bothering him. He took the next turning left off Sheffield Road on to Creesforth Road and travelled up to the last house next to the green belt, The Hacienda. He drove through the open gates, along the short drive round the fountain and stopped directly in front of the stone steps leading up to the front door. He was about to get out of the BMW when he became aware of the arrival of another car behind him.

It was a swish red Italian sports car coming round the fountain at speed.

In his driving mirror, he saw it advance towards him from behind. It was travelling much faster than he liked. He gasped and braced himself for a collision. Then suddenly it slowed abruptly and stopped only a truncheon's thickness from his rear bumper. He blew out a lungful of air, leaped out of the car and turned round to confront the driver.

A pair of long, nylon clad legs swung out of the low car on to the tarmac. They belonged to Jazmin Frazer.

She laughed as his face showed that he had not appreciated her driving.

'Good afternoon, Inspector.'

'Good afternoon, Miss Frazer,' he said.

'You needn't have worried,' she said. 'There are little cameras at the front and the back of the car so that I can see exactly how near I am to things … an absolute godsend when parking. So sorry if I alarmed you.'

She hadn't hit his car, so there was no problem. He shrugged and said: 'I need to ask you a few questions.'

'Certainly. Come in.'

She unlocked the door pushed it open, threw her shopping and handbag on to the hall table, cancelled the alarm buzzer and directed him into a large comfortable-looking room with easy chairs, sofas and low tables arranged in a semicircle around a giant television screen.

They settled in chairs adjacent to each other. She turned to face him.

'Did Charles Pleasant leave a will?' he said.

'Yes, Inspector. The will is with his solicitors, and, before you ask, he left everything to me, as he promised he would.'

'And have you any idea what his estate amounts to?'

'Not yet. The solicitors are working on it. I believe your Sergeant Taylor took some documents away with him, to do a valuation.'

Angel nodded and wondered if he should tell her the news about the shares and the bonds. He chickened out for the moment and rubbed his lips with his fingers thoughtfully.

'You went to see Larry Longley recently … nine days ago, actually.'

She arched her eyebrows. 'You've been checking up on me.'

'It came up in the course of inquiries.'

'I heard he was ill. I had not seen him since that last day in court. It was four years ago.'

'When he was sentenced to prison.'

'Yes.'

'You attended the trial?'

'Every day. It was awful.'

'Tell me about it.'

She hesitated. After a few moments she said, 'That prosecuting barrister, Twelvetrees … going through all that … evidence … in such graphic detail … that so-called forensic expert … demonstrating with that chopper making such a … big production of it. It was horrible. And cruel.'

'Yes. As a result of all that, I thought you might have hated your brother-in-law?'

'I hated that Twelvetrees and the judge more,' she said. 'It was my sister they were talking about. I know she was a bit of a trollop. And she treated Larry very badly, but they talked about her as if she was … a parcel.'

Angel thought a moment, then said, 'The barrister had to demonstrate to the jury the horror of it, to show what a … monster, the murderer, Larry Longley, was.'

She winced at the word 'murderer'.

'Did you ever meet Larry Longley, Inspector?' she said.

'No. Can't say that I did. The case was dealt with by my previous chief, Detective Chief Inspector Minto, who retired from the force about three years ago. I wasn't in any way involved in it.'

'Well, if you had met Larry Longley, you'd have felt sorry for him. Allowing my sister to behave like that under his nose and in front of their young son, Abe. Larry almost encouraged her, made it easy for her… to carry on with Charles, I mean. Emlyn wouldn't have tolerated it. In fact, when I left Emlyn to go to Charles, Emlyn stood up to me, fought for me, made all sorts of sickening threats against Charles and me. It was only when he could see it was a *fait accompli* that he accepted it and agreed to a divorce. A divorce, I might add, that didn't cost him a penny.'

'Are you saying that Larry Longley was … weak?'

'He had no spirit, Inspector. The doctor at the trial said that he was physically strong and in good health. Being a butcher all those years. Humping all that meat about, I suppose. No. He was weak with people … let my sister, Bridie, walk all over him.'

'Until he wouldn't stand anymore, I suppose?' he said. 'Then he suddenly let out all the accumulated stifled hatred he had been storing up.'

'That's what the psychiatrist said.'

Angel nodded. 'That's what psychiatrists always say.'

They stared at each other.

Angel added: 'But you don't believe it, do you?'

Her mouth dropped open.

Angel continued. 'Then they usually say something like: "The monster crept up on her from behind and when she least expected it, he hit her brutally with a blunt instrument." Did that prosecuting barrister, Twelvetrees, say something like that?'

She didn't answer. She looked afraid. She put a clenched fist to her mouth.

He stared into her eyes. 'Did he?' Angel said. 'Did he say something like that?'

'Yes. Yes. I think he did.'

'You can bet your life, he did,' Angel said, his eyes shining. 'And then it probably went something like this … Twelvetrees might have said, "She instantly fell down dead. Then the evil monster, Longley, carried her to another place, and with a chopper taken from his place of work, chopped her up into pieces, put her in an oil drum, shoved it in the back of a lorry and drove the lorry a hundred miles down the A1. Then, when he thought he was safe, he lowered the tailgate of the lorry, pushed the oil drum off and drove away." Isn't that what he said? Or something like that.'

'Oh yes,' she cried. Her cheeks were wet. Her face was red. 'Yes. Yes,' she muttered into a wet tissue.

He gave her three seconds to wipe her eyes, then he went in for the kill. He spoke each word clearly and deliberately. '*But it wasn't true, was it?*'

'No,' she screamed. 'It wasn't. It wasn't. It wasn't,' she cried. It seemed to come out as if it was a relief to speak out at last. 'He didn't do it. I *now* know he didn't do it.'

'It was Charles Pleasant who murdered Bridie, wasn't it?'

'Yes, but I didn't know that at the time. I only found that out last Tuesday. The day before I went to visit Larry. That's five days before Charles was murdered. He told me. We were having a row about money. Our rows were always about money. It got very heated. He said that I'd have to cut down. He was always saying that. He'd been saying it for years. This time, though, he seemed to mean it. He was very insistent about it. He said some very cruel things. I got quite hurt, angry and distracted and I threatened to leave him. He said he'd kill me if I ever even attempted it. I ridiculed the idea and said what nonsense. Then he said that he'd done it before, he could do it again.'

He kept his eyes on her. She shuddered as if a blast of Arctic air had suddenly blown through the room.

'If he said it to frighten me, he certainly succeeded,' she said. 'I knew *exactly* what he was referring to.'

Angel sighed. The truth had at last been told. A statement from Jazmin Frazer would be enough to take to a judge to make a prima facie case for an unsafe sentence or at the very least grounds for a retrial. In the light of the new evidence, it was possible that Larry Longley could be released from prison shortly.

'Would you be prepared to make a statement to that effect, Miss Frazer?'

'I must. Oh yes. I wouldn't have let Larry go to prison for something Charles had done,' she said. 'That man Twelvetrees put up what seemed to be a strong case … with that doctor and the psychiatrist and all those witnesses. And the police finding the butcher's chopper with his fingerprints on the handle and Bridie's blood on the blade, buried in his back garden….'

'What about the defence?'

'Larry had a barrister, of course. A Mr Bloomfield, I think his name was. He spoke well enough. But he didn't produce many witnesses. The most prominent was Larry's employer who I remember spoke up for him. A big man. His name was Adolphe Hellman. He was wonderful.'

Angel's head came up and his eyes brightened momentarily. That name, Hellman, had cropped up very recently. He was the man who now owned The Hacienda and to whom Pleasant had been paying £800 a week for the privilege of living there. He wondered if she knew?

'Can you remember what he said?'

'He spoke in glowing terms about how good a worker he was, how honest he was, what a good timekeeper, how he got on well at his butcher's business, but that he was quiet and kept himself to himself. I remember he was asked about his personality, and Mr Hellman said that his personality, in his view, didn't match the requirement of a murderer or something like that.'

'I shouldn't think Mr Twelvetrees would like that.'

'From memory, he called the psychiatrist back, and nullified everything that Mr Hellman had said.'

He nodded. That's how the game was played. He rubbed his chin thoughtfully a few times, then he said: 'You saw Larry Longley about a week ago. In Wakefield prison?'

She looked down, licked her lips and said: 'Yes.'

'How was he?'

'It was the first of August. He was very quiet. Very withdrawn. I couldn't get anything much out of him ... just a few nods and grunts ... nothing more. I tried to cheer him up. It was a waste of time. I think he's very ill.'

Angel's lips tightened back against his teeth. 'We've got to get him out of there. Time is of the essence.' He looked at his watch. It was 4.30. 'We need to get back to the station for you to make a formal statement that will start the wheels turning.'

'Oh yes, Inspector,' she said with a sigh.

CHAPTER 15

He had a warm feeling of compassion towards Larry Longley, as well as the heady feeling of playing a leading role in the beginning of the restoration of justice to him and the ill-fated Longley family. The emotion was still with him as he arrived home, closed the back door and turned the key.

He was greeted by the satisfying smell of sizzling beef fat and the sound of bubbling from vegetable pans on the oven top.

Mary was by the sink, rinsing a serving spoon under the tap. She turned when she heard the door close. 'You're early.'

He stepped past the steamy oven, leaned over and gave her a peck on the cheek.

She smiled then blinked. 'You've got the murderer.'

'No,' he said as opened the fridge and took out a beer.

She frowned. 'You've arrested the gang that robbed the bank,' she said, passing him a glass tumbler from the drainer on the worktop.

'No.' He poured out the beer.

She looked at him with her lips half formed into a smile. 'Harker's taken a job in … Tasmania?'

He knew Mary was ribbing him, but he couldn't smile. There was nothing funny about Horace Harker. He took a trial sip of the beer, swallowed it, then took a good swig.

'No,' he said. 'I'm going to get an innocent man out of prison.'

She turned to face him square on, opened her eyes widely and said, 'Really?'

He told her about the interview and the facts that led up to the voluntary statement from Jazmin Frazer. She was impressed and pleased, and listened to the details. They chatted through the meal about the consequences and change to the status quo and then she said, 'But will her evidence assist you in finding Charles Pleasant's murderer?'

He frowned then said, 'It might highlight the suspects.'

She thought for a moment as she swallowed to clear her mouth. Then she said, 'Well, who are they?'

Angel looked up from an enticing piece of beef that wouldn't come away from the bone, wondering if she was really serious.

'The prime suspect would be Emlyn Jones, wouldn't it?' she said. 'When Bridie Longley was murdered, her sister, Jazmin Jones, as she was known at the time, left Emlyn and moved in with Pleasant. He would be bound to hate Pleasant as a consequence.'

'Yeah,' he said. 'But he's got a 24-carat alibi: the photograph with the super, taken by his son, Stanley.'

'And the clock showing the time at 4.30.'

'The clock at 4.30. His son, Stanley, would have been a suspect too. He wouldn't have liked his mother hopping off to Charles Pleasant, would he? And it was Stanley who took the photograph, so he couldn't have shot him either. The super saw him and positively confirms it.'

'Who else? What about Abe Longley? He was Bridie and Larry Longley's son, wasn't he?'

'He would be the next most likely suspect, but I've just seen him. He's got a watertight alibi. He was with his girlfriend and her parents at the time of the murder. Then there's Grant Molloy. The man who worked for Pleasant. He was fiddling Pleasant. I don't know if Pleasant knew about it, or what their relationship was like. But he was downright dishonest. He even found his way into Pleasant's hidden safe.'

'He stole the jade head, didn't he?'

'Well, yes, he did, but he couldn't have murdered Pleasant either. His foot didn't fit the plaster cast.'

'Oh.' She was quiet for a moment as she cut away a mouthful of apple pie with her fork and spoon.

'Mmmm. Who else?'

Angel had just pushed in a large spoonful of the apple pie and was trying to chew it out of the way so that he could reply.

'There's Jazmin herself,' Mary said.

His eyebrows shot up. They came down slowly and turned into a frown. He chewed quickly and swallowed. 'Couldn't be her,' he said. 'Her foot wouldn't fit the plaster cast.'

He put the spoon and fork in the dish and pushed it away.

They had finished the meal. Mary poured the coffee thoughtfully and they carried it through to the sitting room.

When they were settled she said, 'Michael, are you sure about that footprint? Are you sure it is the murderer's?'

'I'm sure of nothing, love, but the range and direction of the bullets fired at Pleasant fit; the used shells ejected from the gun were found on the soft earth of the dug up road, exactly in the place where they would have fallen if a right-handed man in his bare feet had been standing there and had fired a handgun.'

'So you know the murderer was right-handed?'

'He must have been.'

She frowned. 'You keep saying "he".'

'Because the plaster cast is of a man's foot.'

'Oh. I see.'

They drank the coffee in silence for a few moments, then Mary said, 'I've been thinking.'

Angel wrinkled his nose.

'If Larry Longley didn't murder his wife,' she said, 'how did that chopper come to be found buried in his garden?'

'Obviously it was planted there. Expecting the police to find it. That was the crux of the whole case. That's what finally made the jury bring in a guilty verdict.'

'Well, how did it get there?'

'I don't know.'

'If you find that out, you're one step nearer to finding out who murdered Charles Pleasant, aren't you?'

Angel frowned. He was thinking about what Mary had said.

'Well,' she said impatiently. 'What do you think?'

'I was thinking … is there any more apple pie?'

It was 8.35 on Friday the 10th when Angel pulled up at Hellman's giant butcher shop on St George's Road. He stepped inside the brightly illuminated, mirror, glass, chrome and white ceramic emporium, where meat of every shape and texture was displayed seductively under gleaming clear glass. Fifteen men and women dressed in white overalls and hats ran hither and thither up to the long counter and back to the huge cutting and refrigeration area under the watchful eye of a big man seated at a high desk in a glass case strategically placed at the far end of the uncommonly long counter.

Customers were efficiently and pleasantly served and for them, there was no hanging around.

Angel showed his identity to one of the young men in white, who tracked down and along behind the long counter to the end to consult with the big man in the glass case. He looked over the half glasses at Angel who stood patiently amid animated customers, mostly women, thrusting, pointing and questioning the long-suffering and hygienically attired men and women in white.

The young man returned and directed Angel out of the shop door and up the outside of the building to a side door that was opened as he arrived by the big man himself.

'Inspector Angel?' he said, red faced and breathing heavily. 'You want to see me? Come on through.'

He led the way into a small but impressive-looking office. He slumped into a big chair behind a desk and pointed to a chair facing him.

Angel began speaking as soon as he sat down. 'You're Adolphe Hellman. You have two shops, a stall in the market, you sell fresh meat to most of the schools in Bromersley, and pre-packed sandwiches and some prepared meals to the Cheapo chain of supermarkets.'

'That's right,' Hellman said.

'You import tinned and fresh meat products as well as salad items from abroad.'

'Huh,' he snorted. 'You have been through my books.'

'No, but I've been through Charles Pleasant's books,' Angel said looking straight into the bloodshot eyes.

'Oh?' Hellman said. He didn't look pleased. His thick eyebrows lowered and he took out a big spotless handkerchief and wiped it across his forehead.

'Also, you used to employ Larry Longley?'

'I did.'

'And you came to his defence when he was accused of murdering his wife, Bridie, when things looked very black for him.'

'I did. Indeed, I did. By the way, Inspector, I should say that figures alone do not tell the complete story.'

'And it was from your shop that he took the chopper that he used to hack Bridie Frazer's body to pieces.'

'Apparently. Yes. He must have done.'

'No, he didn't,' Angel said.

Hellman's head came up. His jaw dropped. He blinked, held up his hands then frowned.

'Now, you own Charles Pleasant's house,' Angel said. 'The Hacienda.'

'I do. What are you getting at, Inspector?'

'For which you paid only £50,000.'

'Ah. Yes.' He held up a finger quickly and added, 'But there's a reason for that.'

'What is it?'

'He was extremely short of money.'

'That doesn't make sense. You owed him a fortune, for the transport of your imported goods, from London to here. You didn't pay him for months. It added up to a pretty figure.'

'I owed everybody. It is difficult making a profit in the butchering business, Inspector. Staff wages. Competition from the multiples. Health and Safety regulations. Ministry of this, that and the other. Foot and mouth. It's hell, I tell you.'

'At the same time as you owed him all this money, the Frazer sisters were milking him at a colossal rate.'

He shook his head. He didn't know what to say. He waved the handkerchief at him. 'I'm not responsible for what the Frazer girls got up to.'

'He was paying you eight hundred pounds a week. What was that for?'

His jaw stiffened. He clenched his hands. 'Look, I don't have to answer these questions. I haven't done anything wrong.'

'If you refuse to answer I can arrest you for obstructing police with their inquiries.'

He groaned. 'Rent. Rent on The Hacienda.'

'Eight hundred pounds a week?'

'Yes. I own it. It's worth it. I am entitled to ask whatever rent I like.'

'But you only paid £50,000 for the house. Laughably, the surviving Frazer sister, Jazmin, will be the one paying you the outrageous sum of eight hundred a week for the privilege of living in what she currently believes is her house. She doesn't know that Charles Pleasant sold it from under her nose and that you are her landlord. Wait till she finds that out!'

Hellman held his hands in the air. 'One has to do one's best.'

'I suppose that amounts to taking advantage of a man in financial difficulty.'

'I was the one in financial difficulty, Inspector Angel. Me. Adolphe Hellman! Charles Pleasant? No. Never. His father left him a thriving metal retrieving business, and he sold his own transport business for a seven-figure sum, I believe. I bought the house to help him out. We both had cashflow problems. The butchering business … I have told you, it is difficult to make a profit. I still have a cash flow problem. Even now. Yes. A big cash flow problem. Do you know what the total council tax bill is for my properties?'

'You owed Charles Pleasant so much money for transporting your stuff from the London docks and Smithfield market that he could have bankrupted you if he had issued a writ for the money you owed him?'

'Yes. Well, at the time, maybe,' he said as he wiped his fat red neck with the sticky handkerchief. 'I wouldn't want the world to know that. It is not good for business.'

Angel rubbed his chin thoughtfully for a few seconds, then his eyelids rose up and then down. 'So when Charles Pleasant suggested that you gave him Larry Longley's chopper straight from the position in the shop where he had last put it, you agreed.'

Hellman's face went scarlet. 'I did not agree,' he said. 'I wouldn't have betrayed an employee like that. It's disgraceful that you should suggest such a thing. I loved that man.'

'If you didn't give him the chopper, then you must have been the murderer of Bridie Frazer.'

'I murdered nobody. What are you trying to do to me?'

'Be sensible, Mr Hellman. If you didn't murder her, then Charles Pleasant must have done. In which case, how did he get hold of the chopper?'

'I don't know. He didn't. I mean, it was Larry Longley who—'

'You left it somewhere where Charles Pleasant could easily have helped himself to it.'

'This is outrageous! I want my solicitor. I am entitled to have my solicitor present.'

Angel jumped to his feet. 'Yes, sir. You are,' he said. 'Come with me down to the station. We'll record all this and we'll have your solicitor in, and do all this officially … on the record.'

Hellman looked up at the ceiling and rubbed his chin vigorously. He remained seated and said, 'I have just remembered; I can't. I am expecting a big delivery of beef carcasses. I need to check them before they are unloaded.'

Angel slowly sat down again. 'Let's not play games, Mr Hellman. If you didn't kill Bridie Frazer, you know who did. And it was the person you let have Larry Longley's chopper.'

Hellman's bottom lip quivered.

Angel stared into his eyes. 'It was Charles Pleasant, wasn't it,' he said.

Hellman gave the very slightest nod, then quickly turned his bloodshot eyes away from Angel's penetrating gaze.

Angel now knew the truth. He licked his lips and said, 'You must know that the finding of the chopper buried in his own garden with Bridie's blood still on it proved to be the vital evidence that sealed Larry Longley's fate.'

'No. I know nothing about it,' Hellman said weakly.

'After Charles Pleasant had murdered her, he dumped her in the scrapyard, took the chopper from here, hewed her to pieces, then buried the weapon in Larry Longley's garden. He put her remains in an old oil drum and transported it in one of his lorries down the A1.'

Hellman covered his face with his handkerchief. 'I know nothing about it, I tell you,' he wailed uselessly. 'I stuck up for Larry in the witness box. I gave him an excellent reference. I even said he wasn't disposed to any kind of violence. He was a lovely man. Why are you telling all these lies?'

Angel sighed. He rubbed his chin. It wasn't difficult to ignore Hellman's pleas.

Angel sniffed and then said, 'After that, blackmail was easy, wasn't it? The rent is actually disguised blackmail, isn't it? To buy your silence. £800 a week is outrageous, but the plan was that next year it would have been £1,000 and the year after that £2,000 and so on, ad infinitum. That's how you planned it to work, didn't you? What a wickedly cruel, brilliant plan. You're a blackmailer. It was the formula for a most wonderful pension for you in your old age, wasn't it? Better than any insurance company could have devised. But, alas, the plan went wrong. Something you never thought of. A real bombshell. The rich sucker was murdered and, sadly for me, I can't prove one word of your involvement in the wrongful imprisonment of Larry Longley and this subsequent despicable crime. Sadly for you, Mr Hellman, blackmail is not transferable. You will slowly sink in your own mire.'

The station was hectic when Angel returned. Such a lot of coming and going. Phones were going like voting on *The X Factor*.

He put his head into the CID office; Ahmed saw him and came to the door. 'Did you get hold of DS Crisp, lad?'

'He's coming in straightaway, sir. And he said to tell you that the woman is Chantelle Moses. She does have a mole on her right temple.'

Angel frowned. It didn't seem to matter now. 'Right. What about everybody else?'

'Everybody should be here, sir. I said ten o'clock. The Operations Room should be empty. DC Scrivens is behind you.'

Scrivens came running up. His face as sad as a Strangeways dumpling. 'Good morning, sir,' he said. Then he looked down at the floor.

Angel got the message. 'Never mind, lad. So you didn't find the ambulance. The trouble is, these robbers are far too smart for us. It will have been transformed into a dodgem car and sold on to Alton Towers, I expect, by now. Never mind. Come on. We have other fish to fry.'

Scrivens looked up and gave a weak smile: the tension had gone.

Angel bustled down to the Operations Room followed by the other two. He opened the door and looked inside. It was empty.

'This'll do for us,' he said.

It was the size, and similarly arranged to, a school classroom. There were local maps and blackboards on the walls and flip charts on easels and twenty-five or so chairs facing a raised platform.

Ahmed said, 'By the way, sir. The number on the fake ambulance was for a bus in Wiltshire. I didn't pursue it.'

'It's what I expected. Ta.'

Gawber joined them. 'Sit down everybody,' Angel said.

There was a knock on the door and Crisp arrived.

Angel said, 'Ah. Glad you were following the right woman, lad. Anything new there?'

'She still spending money, sir. Clothes, shoes, hairdos.'

Angel nodded. 'Right, Trevor. Take a pew.'

Angel looked round. All he had summoned were there. 'I've called you all together to see if we can put our communal mind together and make some progress in this bare foot murder business … the murder of Charles Pleasant. I want to put a few facts to you and see if we can make any sense of the thing. Feel free to butt in if anything occurs to you. Now, there are a few unusual factors in this case that I haven't come across before. One, it seems apparent that Pleasant, although he had a scrap metal business employing one man, Grant Molloy, he was actually making his money through dealing in stolen valuables or works of art … expensive pieces … well, relatively expensive pieces.'

'The jade head was worth millions, sir,' Gawber said. 'Wasn't it?'

'Yes, Ron. But I shouldn't think he paid millions for it.'

'No, but couldn't he have been murdered for it,' Crisp said.

'I shouldn't have thought so. A man called Goldstein died for it and it was at any rate returned to its rightful owner, the Empress of somewhere or other. But you have brought me to the point about motive. He was found with £8,000 in notes on him.'

'So he was going to buy something, sir?' Scrivens said.

'We have to assume that … yes. Whatever it was, I suppose we may never find out. It doesn't matter anyway. We know that somebody phoned him that Sunday morning, and set up a meeting at the scrapyard, we believe, for 4.30 in the afternoon. Although, as we know, Pleasant arrived early at 4.18 or 4.19, and he was shot dead at about 4.19.'

'Can we not find out who it was from the phones?' Gawber said.

'Don Taylor's checked out Jazmin Frazer's. Come to think, she'd hardly be phoning the man she's living with. We have had no success there. If we had enough evidence, we could check out the other suspects' phones. But I expect that a pay-as-you-go mobile was bought specifically for the job. The one call was made and the phone slung into the River Don.

'Now, the caller who set up the meeting would know that Pleasant would have £8,000 on him, but no attempt at robbery was made. His pockets had not been rifled. The money was intact. That indicates that the murderer wasn't interested primarily in financial gain. This murder was about something else. It has to be revenge or … retaliation or fear. There are a few people who had cause to hate him, but before going there, I'd like to remind you of some of the peculiarities of this case. Firstly, the murderer was bare foot. Secondly, the victim had no shoes on. And thirdly, there are no prints on the car door handle, yet Pleasant wasn't wearing gloves. Why would he want to wipe it clean of prints if, indeed, he did?'

The men looked at each other, but nobody made to say anything.

Angel passed his hand through his hair. 'Why shoot a man in your bare feet? What's the point?'

There were a few mutters of, 'Don't know, sir,' and shaking of heads.

'We don't seem to know, sir,' Gawber said.

Angel nodded. 'No. And neither do I.'

He continued. 'There also seems to be an inconsistency in the information I got from the manager and his wife at the lodging house. One of them happened to mention that they had a dog and a kennel. I looked round there two days ago and there was no sign of either, nor was there any mess in the yard or any giveaway signs of that sort. In itself it's not at all important, but if there isn't a dog why lie about it. If there is a dog, where is it? Anyway, next Sunday, I am making a point of being at the scene of crime at the vital time and I'll take the opportunity of speaking to them about it then … try and clear it up.'

There were more nods all round.

'Well, let's move on to the suspects, then,' Angel said. 'Let's see if we can throw any new light there.'

'Grant Molloy is a thoroughly dishonest piece,' Gawber said.

'He is, but—' Angel said rubbing his chin.

'There's Emlyn Jones and his son,' Crisp said. 'And Abe Longley. And Jazmin Frazer.'

'Yes,' Angel said. 'Yes. And there's one other. Adolphe Hellman.'

He reported the interview he'd had with that morning with the butcher and told them in detail about the supplying of the chopper to Pleasant, the murder of Bridie Frazer by Pleasant and the subsequent blackmail by Hellman.

'We can't get him for the blackmail,' he said, 'but thankfully it died when Charles Pleasant died. However, Pleasant was obviously becoming strapped for cash. Hellman and the Frazer women had almost picked him clean. Pleasant could have been desperate, resented paying the blackmail, threatened to expose the big man, who shot him dead to save his own skin. He has no alibi for Sunday afternoon. He was at home by himself, avoiding the sun and trying to keep cool.'

Angel looked round to see if anybody had any comment to make. There was nothing.

'To sum up then,' he continued, 'we know from the footprint that the murderer is a man, so it couldn't be Jazmin Frazer. Abe Longley has an alibi from three good people. The annoying thing is that I am convinced that Jones and his son Stanley knew the arrangements, the time at least of the murder, yet they seem to have the perfect alibi. We have been unable to break it. That only leaves Adolphe Hellman.'

CHAPTER 16

The remainder of that Friday seemed to have been wasted in a morass of pointless paperwork and blind alley inquiries. Angel was glad to get home. It was the weekend. Two days out of the office. There were no fireworks nor interesting or exciting plans to look forward to there, just the humdrum business of living, eating, shopping and keeping house. He dutifully went with Mary to the supermarket on Saturday afternoon and spent Sunday morning and the early afternoon in the garden, cutting the lawn and weeding the borders. At three o'clock, he put the tools away, had a wash and put on his office suit. He came down the stairs through the hall to the kitchen.

Mary was at the sink filling the kettle. She heard him approaching and turned round. She saw the suit, looked him up and down, pulled a face and said, 'What's this then? Going somewhere?'

He expected a certain amount of disapproval. That's why he hadn't mentioned it. Mary believed that he should not be working between 5.30 p.m. on a Friday and 8.30 a.m. on a Monday morning.

He had other ideas.

'Yes. I'm going up to Sebastopol Terrace. It's a week today since—'

‘I remember,’ she said. ‘It spoiled a most beautiful day. We were in the garden. Quite the sunniest day for years. Ruined.’

‘Won’t be long.’

He escaped without any further censure.

He parked the BMW outside ‘the rooms to let’ lodging house, next to the hole in the road and facing Charles Pleasant’s scrapyard. Everything looked the same as it had done a week ago. Strange and eerie. He got out of the car and the rowdy racket from that hideous radio met his ears again. His face muscles tightened. After a peaceful day at home he had a great desire to get that teenage girl and her rattle box and throw them both off Flamborough Head into the sea.

He braced himself, stepped into the lodging house, went up to the counter and pressed the bell. As before, the racket stopped, the door opened and the man with the face of a ferret, Samson Tickle, came out. He needed a shave.

He looked up at the policeman. The pupils of his eyes grew bigger momentarily. ‘It’s Inspector Angel, isn’t it? What brings you back, Inspector?’ he said, looking away and fidgeting with a book on the counter.

Angel gave him one of his searching looks. ‘I think you know, Mr Tickle.’

‘Ah, well, I didn’t realize that it would matter.’

Angel frowned. He didn’t know what he was talking about. He stopped frowning but maintained the gaze.

‘I mean the working girls round here can’t afford much. When they bring their clients they only take the room for an hour or so, we can’t charge them much, we never thought it mattered. Commercial travellers don’t want their firms knowing they stay here, at a quarter the cost their expense chitties say. But if I was to make a show of booking them in, they would shy away for fear of being caught out fiddling their expenses. That’s the whole point. Their firms think that they’re staying at a much more expensive place. The idea of putting it through the books … why, they would stop coming altogether. Don’t you see that, Inspector?’

Angel only had a slight grasp on what he was saying. He decided to clear one thing at once. 'Where is the dog you had last Sunday and where is its kennel?'

Tickle's jaw dropped. 'What did you say?'

'Have you a dog in the house?'

'No, sir. No pets allowed in the rooms. No dogs, cats, budgerigars, snakes—'

'Last Sunday you said you had a dog. I thought it was your dog. Somebody mentioned a kennel?'

Tickle frowned, then he smiled; at least Angel took it for a smile. He was one of the few people in the world, like Gordon Brown, who couldn't smile. It made him look as if he was about to throw up. 'I remember,' he said. 'That was the wife, Inspector.'

Angel rubbed his forehead gently with two fingers. 'Please explain.'

'We don't have no dog. Never had no dog, Inspector. Whenever there's a puddle of water anywhere, my wife pretends it's a dog having cocked up its leg when it shouldn't have. It's a polite way, she says, of explaining away any water leaks or spillages.'

Angel's face brightened. 'You had some leaks or spillages on the landing, I recall?'

Tickle looked away quickly.

'How did they get there?' Angel said.

'There were a few puddles of water on the landing, I believe. Nothing much.'

'How did they get there?'

'All right, Inspector. All right. They were the result of some yob who had left his shower on.'

'But you said you had nobody staying with you.'

'We hadn't at the time. He had left earlier.'

'What time?'

'Don't know. Didn't see him go. Left the water running. Water running down the chandelier rose in the drawing room.'

'Didn't you think of reporting it to the police?'

'We're used to that sort of carry on, Inspector. We can't do nothing about it. Anyway, what could we possibly have charged him with, wasting water?'

Angel sighed.

'He even left his underwear,' Tickle said. 'Even left his shoes with his socks still stuck in them.'

Angel's pulse began thumping. 'Where are they?'

'What?'

'Shoes. And socks. And underwear.'

Tickle wrinkled his ferret-like nose. 'Incinerator. They weren't nice.'

Angel's face went scarlet. 'Show me the room he was in.'

Tickle went round the counter and up the dark staircase. Angel followed. They passed several doors each side and ended at the last door, which was open.

Angel followed him into the room. It was clean, basic and altogether satisfactory. It smelled of beeswax. There was a modern power shower in the corner. Clean towel on a towel stand. A window looked out on to the road in front. He looked down at the scrapyard and nodded knowingly.

'The wife's cleaned it out thoroughly, of course.'

Angel sniffed. She appeared to have made a good job of it too. He wasn't pleased.

They returned downstairs to the counter.

'What did the man look like?'

'I didn't really notice. Just ordinary. Average, you might say.'

'Had he any distinguishing features? Tattoos? Was he tall, short, fat, thin?'

'Just average, I'd say.'

'Bald, thick head of hair, red, blonde, white?'

'Just average.'

'Would you recognize him if you saw him again? If I showed you photographs—'

'Shouldn't think so. He kept his head down as he passed his money over.'

'What did he pay?'

'Ten pounds. Everybody pays ten pounds. He paid me with a ten-pound note.'

'Have you still got it?'

He sniggered. 'Shouldn't think so. Money comes and goes, you know.'

Angel's jaw stiffened. 'What time did he arrive?'

'About three o'clock, maybe later. He didn't stay long.'

'What did he say?'

'Just that he'd like to rest a few hours ... keep out of the sun. How much? I said ten pounds. Choose any room you like and close the door. That's what I always say. He paid and went up the stairs. It took less time than I took to tell you. That's all I know.'

'Did your wife or your daughter see him?'

'No. Why? Who was he?'

'He was the murderer of Charles Pleasant.'

Tickles face went white.

Angel checked his watch. It was 4.15 p.m. He left the little man recovering behind the counter, and stepped out of the lodging house into the sunshine. It was still a pleasant day but nothing like as hot as it had been the same time the previous week. He glanced back at the scrapyard. The gates were locked and everywhere was silent. Just as he expected it would have been the previous Sunday. It was spooky. The raucous racket from the lodging house started up again. He started walking down Sebastopol Terrace away from the scrapyard and away from the noise. Nobody was about. One might have expected children to be out playing ball games or hop scotch or similar. Nobody was out scrubbing their step, washing their windows or painting the gate. He continued his way towards the junction of Bradford Road. In the distance, but very loudly, he heard the chime of an ice cream van. 'Half a pound of tuppeny rice, Half a pound of treacle'. A few seconds later, it turned the corner and stopped at the junction. The driver parked up, switched off the chime. Angel was about a hundred yards away. He made a beeline for him. Several people rushed out of their houses and formed a short queue. The driver served them quickly and everybody disappeared as quickly as they had appeared. The salesman was about to close the serving window, when he saw Angel approach. He held up a finger to catch his attention.

He flashed his warrant card and made himself known.

'Were you here about this time last Sunday?'

The salesman said, 'Yes, I was.'

'A man was murdered, shot in his car outside the scrap-yard at the far end of the street. Did you see anything at all?'

His eyebrows went up. 'No, mate. I was pulled off my feet last Sunday. It was the hottest day for fifteen years. I had to go back to the depot three times for a fill up. My takings was up ten times what I usually take. Everybody worked sixteen hours, flat out. They made part-timers into full-timers. We was that busy. I would like to help. I didn't see nothing.'

'Anybody running away, any cars, anything unusual? Anybody in bare feet?'

'Bare feet?' He blinked then shook his head.

He saw nothing at all unusual last Sunday on his travels.

Angel thanked him.

The ice cream van rattled on up the hill.

Angel turned round and walked at an easy pace the length of Sebastopol Terrace, past his car and up to the scra-pyard gates. He looked at the piles of metal rubbish through the bars. He felt uncomfortable as the critical time of 4.19 passed. He had to be there. Something or somebody might have caused something to happen. But nothing did.

He glanced down the long row of terraced houses until just after 4.30, then returned to his car, unable to avoid the hideous racket emanating from speakers in the lodging house.

He was home for 4.40. He put the car in the garage, locked up and went in the bungalow.

Mary was at the sink washing a lettuce. She gave him a sideways glance.

'I'll make you a cup of tea, in a minute.'

'Ta, love.'

She sighed. 'You can't leave that job alone, can you? Whatever will you do when they make you retire?'

'I'll cross that bridge when I get to it.'

'If you get to it.'

They had tea and then watched television. There was *Songs of Praise*, followed by a re-run of *Last of the Summer Wine*, then the titles came on for one of those eighteenth-century classical costume plays.

Mary was delighted and settled back in her chair with a contented expression.

Angel yawned when he saw what he was in for. He'd seen the like before … an overpublicized, expensive production incorporating a brigade of famous actresses and actors, the men in tight pants and the women fluttering up and down in big hats, saying things like, 'Mamma, I do declare that Mr Clothhooly looks very handsome on a horse.' 'Mamma, do you think the vicar will bring the new curate for tea?' 'Mamma, Sir John Finglechomp wants to speak to Papa (sob sob). O Mamma, dear Mamma, I really he think wants to ask Papa permission to take my hand in holy matricide.' He yawned again.

Mary poured him and herself a second cup of tea without taking her eyes off the screen.

For Angel, the film was destined to send him to sleep. He expected it to begin with a funeral and a flock of people returning to a big house and removing their coats and hats. And it did! Then he saw something that caught his attention. It wasn't that unusual. At that time, even insignificant. A woman with a gigantic hat pin. It looked about 10" long. She looked quite dangerous with it. She took it out of the hat so that she could take it off. He wondered what she would do with it after she had removed the hat. It reminded him of the collection of hat pins at Jones's shop. This woman stuck the pin back in the hat and put the hat on a table. He wondered. What if she had intended parting with the hat and therefore had had no hat to stick it back into. Supposing she had to transport it somewhere. At Jones's shop, he had a big pincushion to stick it in, but supposing, just supposing, she had wanted to take it upstairs or next door or down the street, or have given it to her 'Dear Mamma, I do declare?' The thing was dangerous. Ten inches of steel with a sharp point. It could be a real weapon. It needed a cover of some sort surely … a holster … a cork at the end might be all right, but it could get knocked off … it needed an all-over cover … like a long sausage shaped thing … a sausage itself wouldn't do … once it's punctured there'd be greasy stuff coming out all over … a French stick … that would be too crumbly … an apple … not long enough … a carrot … yes a carrot … good, but still not quite long enough … a parsnip would be just right … a PARSNIP! He stopped.

He suddenly heard Mary's voice. 'Are you all right, Michael?'

'What?' he said.

'Are you all right? You shouted something.'

'What?'

'You shouted "Parsnip" I thought it was,' she said. 'Are you all right?

He shook his head and looked at her strangely.

'Look,' she said, her fists clenched, 'if you really don't want this, we've got a tape somewhere of Benny Hill.'

'No, love. No,' he said. 'You enjoy it. I will go for … a walk. I want to think something out … I'm all right. You enjoy it. Won't be long. I must go—'

And he was gone.

It was a quarter past nine on Monday morning when Angel pulled up outside The Moo Moo Ice Cream Parlour, Abbeyside Road, Sheffield. The Moo Moo was a well-known short-order café, and of course sold the celebrated Moo Moo ice cream. Staff in their distinctive white overalls flitted from table to table cleaning and clearing in preparation for another busy day. There were only half a dozen customers in there at that time, drinking coffee, as it was so early.

Angel went straight up to the cashier at the paydesk, made himself known and asked to see the manager. A few moments later, a pleasant young man came up to him.

'I'm Roland Markway, shop manager. How can I help you?'

'I'm making inquiries about a Miss Penelope Furnace,' Angel said. 'Does she work here?'

The man smiled. 'She certainly does, Inspector. She's my fiancée.' Then his face changed. 'Is she in any trouble?'

Angel's eyebrows shot up. Now there was a surprise. How many fiancés does she have? He rubbed his chin. 'Is she here now?'

'She's part time. Doesn't start until 10 o'clock. Is there anything wrong?'

'Shouldn't think so, Mr Markway. This is just an inquiry. All I really need to know is whether she was at work here at 4.20 last Sunday afternoon?'

'She certainly was. That was the day of the heatwave.'

The pupils of Angel's eyes rose up and then down. His pulse began to race. This may be the breakthrough he had been looking for. There was an uncontrollable fluttery movement and warmth in his chest, accompanied by a regular thumping of his heart. He always had a reaction like this when he sensed that he was near solving a difficult case. He had been like this ever since he had caught his first murderer as a sergeant in 1988. He hoped that he was able to conceal his excitement from Roland Markway. He took in a deep breath and tried to breathe out slowly and evenly.

'Are you certain?' he said. 'At 4.20?'

'Oh yes. She was here all day from ten o'clock until eight in the evening. Penny worked jolly hard. Everybody was here. Sales were an all-time record. I didn't get home myself until almost eleven o'clock. Is she in any trouble?'

He hesitated before replying. 'No. No,' he said, feigning unhurried serenity and benevolence. It wasn't true, but he had no choice. He didn't want Markway alarming Penny, then her tipping Abe Longley off and him legging it away. Villains can be in Rio de Janeiro in ten hours these days if they have it planned ahead.

Angel thanked the young man, left the café and returned to his car.

Things may be moving at last.

He took out his mobile and tapped in Gawber's number.

'I'm in Sheffield, Ron. Drop everything. Find Scrivens or a PC, bring a plaster cast of the footprint of the murderer – there's one in my office – come over here and see if it fits Abe Longley. If it does, arrest him, book him and take him back with you. He's probably at his flat.'

'Right, sir.'

'According to her boss, who strangely happens to be her boyfriend, Penelope Furnace was working all day Sunday the 5th, serving up ice cream at the time she said she was having tea with him and her parents. Now, if the parents change their tune, we could have our murderer.'

Gawber whooped with joy. 'Great stuff, sir. I'll leave straightaway. We should be there in twenty-five minutes.'

'I'm now going straight to Penny Furnace's parents. See what they have to say. Keep in touch.'

'Right, sir.'

He closed the phone and drove determinedly up Barnsley Road to the flats. He was there in seven minutes. He parked up the BMW, went up the concrete steps and along, passing Abe Longley's flat number 112, to the Furnaces', number 114. He tapped on the door. It was answered by Mrs Furnace. When she saw Angel she smiled but it wasn't the same smile she had greeted him with four days previously.

'Mr Angel? Good morning. What brings you here? I'm afraid our Penny has just stepped out to the shop.'

He looked her straight in the eye and said: 'It's you and your husband I have come to see. May I come in?'

He noticed the looks that were exchanged between the husband and wife as he stepped into the tiny living room. Mr Furnace was sitting in a chair by the fireplace and the television was blaring away, the big slim screen dominating the room. Mrs Furnace invited him to sit by the table and then turned the television off.

'Now what is it, lad?' Mr Furnace said.

'It's about the whereabouts of Abe Longley a week last Sunday, the 5th.'

Mr Furnace rubbed his chin vigorously. Then he looked into his wife's sad eyes and said, 'It's no good, love. We'll have to tell him.'

She nodded.

'It was for our Penelope, really,' she said. 'We wanted what we thought was the very best for her.'

Angel nodded gently and said, 'Of course. Tell me all about it.'

'Well, we wanted her to find a nice young man and settle down. We thought she'd found one. We understood Abe's father had died and left him over a million pounds. He bought us this television set. It's very, very nice, but we thought it was a bit fishy. He doesn't look or seem like a millionaire's son.'

'His father is alive in Wakefield prison, Mrs Furnace. But he is innocent and shouldn't be there. I intend to have his case re-tried. But he isn't a millionaire. Never was. Like his son, he was a butcher.'

'Oh. A butcher? He said his father was dead,' she said and she looked at her husband.

Mr Furnace said, 'He said his father had been a property developer!'

He shook his head. 'The money he's throwing around is part of the proceeds of an armed bank robbery.'

The couple stared at each other open mouthed.

'Oh dear,' Mrs Furnace said. 'I don't know what to say.'

'Well, tell me about that Sunday afternoon, the 5th.'

'Oh dear. Well, he came here all flushed, late that Sunday night. Said that that afternoon, he'd been to a car boot sale, while our Penelope was at work. He said that while he was looking round for a present for her, his car was clamped, and that it was going to cost him £160 to pay to get unclamped. Anyway, he hadn't got the £160 on him. He said he was angry. He said that he had a hacksaw in the boot of his car and managed to remove the clamp and throw it over the hedge. Then he said that if the clamping company found out who he was they could fine him for damaging their clamp. On the other hand, as nobody had actually seen him, he could get away with it if he could say that he was with us. So with pressure from our Penelope, we agreed, but we hadn't realized that … oh dear.'

'Where is your Penelope now?'

The room door opened and she stepped inside. Her face was red, she was wiping her eyes. 'I'm here,' she said. She was wearing the white overall dress with Moo Moo embroidered on the lapels. 'I had a text on my mobile from Roland. I've just rung him. He told me you'd been asking about that Sunday. And I heard it all. Every word.' She looked at Angel. 'No. I wasn't with Abe Longley having tea at 4.30 a week last Sunday. I was down at that rotten ice cream shop, slapping out ice cream sundaes and banana splits till gone ten o'clock.'

Angel nodded.

'Thank you, Penny,' he said. He knew she must be smarting at the embarrassment.

Her mother went over to her, but she shrugged her off.

He was sorry that there had to be so much pain in this business, but he was excited that he'd had confirmation that there was no alibi.

Angel suddenly looked up. 'Does anybody know where Abe Longley will be at the moment?'

'He'll still be in bed,' Penny said as she looked at her watch. 'Oh! I'll be late for work, 'she said. Then her face brightened. She was a different woman. She dashed round the room, gave her mother and father each a quick peck on the cheek, and then crossed to Angel. She stretched up on to her toes and gave him a kiss on the cheek, laughed and went out, closing the door after her.

Angel smiled and dug into his pocket for his mobile.

CHAPTER 17

He arrived home at six o'clock. It had been a busy, tiring day.

Mary was in the sitting room on a lounge chair with her legs up on a matching stool, watching the news on television.

'I'm in here,' she called when she heard the back door close.

'Right, love.'

He came in, leaned over and gave her a kiss.

She smiled at first then her face straightened. 'You've been drinking.'

'I've had a couple in the Fat Duck.'

Her jaw dropped. Then she said, 'You've got somebody for that murder?'

He smiled. 'What's for tea?'

'You've got the gang who robbed the Great Northern Bank?'

'Tell me what's for tea and I'll tell you all about it.'

'It's salmon and salad. It's in the fridge. We can have it whenever we like.'

'Good. Let me get a beer and take my coat off.'

He went into the kitchen and the phone began ringing.

'I'll get it,' he said and came back into the hall.

Mary switched off the television.

He picked up the phone.

It was Ron Gawber.

'What's wrong, Ron?'

'Nothing wrong, sir. Thought you'd like to know that Abe Longley's shooting his mouth off. He's hinted that he knows who did the Great Northern Bank Robbery and he wants to do a deal.'

'No deals, Ron.'

'He wants to tell us how the robbery was done and the names of the gang.'

'I know all that. No deals, Ron. Goodbye.'

There was some hesitation before Gawber said, 'Goodbye, sir.'

He replaced the phone.

Mary heard the clunk. 'Who was that?' she called.

'I'm coming,' he yelled. He grabbed a beer out of the fridge, a glass out of the cupboard and came into the sitting room. 'It was Ron Gawber. A prisoner wanted to grass on his mates and tell us how the robbery was done.'

'You mix with some nice people.'

He poured the beer, took a sip and put it on the coaster.

'So what are you going to do?' she added.

'I know how it was done.'

'Oh? Are you going to tell me then?'

'Of course. You remember that overpumped costume play you saw last night and enjoyed so much.'

'And you didn't. The only part you saw was the beginning. The hat pins.'

'Yes. The hat pins. And last week, I told you about the parsnips I saw in both the Jones' – father and son – houses. Well, I worked out that, as daft as it sounds, a parsnip would be a safe, suitable and cheap holster in which to carry a hatpin around.'

'Mmm. I suppose. Yes, but what for?'

'I'm coming to that. A hat pin would be a very suitable tool with which to puncture the plastic ball cock in a lavatory cistern, which would result in the water seeping into it, causing it slowly to sink and stay sunk. Subsequently, the water filling the cistern would then overflow and flood the place out.'

'The Great Northern Bank?'

'Precisely. All it left for forensic and the plumber was a pinprick in the ballcock. No wonder they were bewildered. All of this dawned on me when I remembered that I had seen a set up in Jones's shop without realizing that that's what he was doing. There were a series of bowls and chamberpots with plastic balls, one in each, some sunk and some floating. He was experimenting with different hat pins, making different diameter holes in rubber balls to determine which hat pin to use to sink a ballcock in a specific length of time. I realized later that it was a timing experiment. I had asked him what they were and he told me some rubbish about checking whether the pots leaked or not. It has been at the back of my mind ever since.'

'He must have a devious mind.'

'Anyway, the robbery worked like this. Chantelle Moses arrived at the bank, padded up as a pregnant woman. She carried a long hat pin safely stuck into a parsnip somewhere on her; also a glass vial containing sulphretted hydrogen stuck to a piece of sticky tape. She conned her way into the lavatory. With the hat pin she made a miniscule hole in the floating plastic ballcock in the cistern, which we now know caused a flood ten minutes after she had been taken away by Stanley Jones and Abe Longley dressed up as ambulance men in charge of a fake ambulance. She placed the vial in the hinge of the door, and she clocked the position and height of the CCTV cameras for her partner and his cousin for when they made their second entrance as plumbers later. The telephone calls, the interceptions and the voices were being appropriately managed by Emlyn Jones on a stool outside the solicitor's office next door to the bank. He was also, of course, the mastermind behind the whole thing. The rest you know. At 6 o'clock tomorrow morning, three of the four of them will be arrested simultaneously, and charged with bank robbery.'

'That's great, Michael. But why only three?'

'Because we already have the fourth in custody charged with murder.'

Her face glowed. 'Really? Well, who is it? And why did he murder him in his bare feet?'

'Well, it was Abe Longley.'

'Really? Abe Longley? I thought he had an alibi with his girlfriend and their parents?'

'It was a lie, and we broke it.'

'But why did he murder him in his bare feet?'

'I'm getting there. I'll tell you.'

'And why was Charles Pleasant driving without shoes?'

Angel smiled. 'In 2003, Jazmin left her husband, Emlyn Jones, to live with Charles Pleasant. Emlyn Jones hated Pleasant for taking her away from him and their son Stanley. Likewise, Larry Longley hated Pleasant for taking his wife, Bridie, away from him and their son, Abe. And I suspect that Jones had for some time egged his nephew on to get even with him. He had said he couldn't himself. As the deserted husband, he'd be bound to be the prime suspect. Anyway, as his father was suffering and getting weaker in prison, Abe must have eventually agreed, a plan made and alibis set in place.

'They knew Pleasant was dealing in stolen valuables, antiquities and so on, so somebody, Jones probably, disguised his voice, phoned Pleasant and made a deal to offer to sell him something interesting for £8,000, and an appointment at the scrapyard for 4.30 p.m. was duly arranged. Now, Emlyn Jones, Stanley and Abe Longley had to have good alibis. Abe had worked hard at creating a relationship with Penny Furnace and her parents, and Emlyn Jones planned to be photographed by his son, with the super, at the Potts gig at 4.30 exactly. It was this exactness that started me thinking. The murder actually occurred ten or eleven minutes earlier than planned. As you remember, it was a very hot summer Sunday afternoon … hottest day for fifteen summers. Anyway, sometime that afternoon, before 4.00, I suppose,

Abe Longley arrived at Sebastopol Terrace … he was early … he had time on his hands … decided to take shelter out of the sun and out of the way of potential witnesses. He rented a room in the lodging house next door to the scrap metal dealer's, which very suitably had a bird's eye view of the yard. It was very hot. He was uncomfortable, maybe he … looked at the time … decided he'd time to take a cool shower. He stripped down and got in the shower. While enjoying the coolness of the water, he heard the sound of a car arriving. He leaped out of the shower, looked through the window, saw the car drive up below … it was Pleasant's Bentley arriving at the scrapyard. He was undressed and wet through. He pulled on his trousers and shirt and grabbed his gun and dashed into street, leaving the room with the shower running and his pants, shoes and anything else behind. The puddles complained about upstairs in the hotel weren't made by water leaks or imagined dogs, they were made by Abe Longley. When he reached the pavement outside the front of the lodging house, Pleasant had already got out of car, unlocked the padlock, pushed open the gate, returned to the car, got in, closed the car door, and was about to drive into the yard. It was at that moment that Longley, in wet clothes and no shoes, arrived. He dodged behind the cement mixer and fired four shots from a gun fitted with a silencer. Pleasant flopped over the steering wheel, dead. Longley then started to run off, he realized he had no shoes. There was nobody around. He didn't want to waste time going back upstairs. So he rushed over to Pleasant's car, opened the car door, removed his shoes, closed the door, wiped the door handle clean of his prints, put on the dead man's shoes and ran off.'

Mary's jaw dropped. 'And that was it?'

Angel nodded.

There was a knock at the door. They looked at each other. They weren't expecting anybody.

'I'll go,' Mary said, pushing herself out of the chair.

'I'm having another beer. Do you want anything?'

'Just a tonic water, love.'

Angel went into the kitchen and opened the cupboard. From the front door, he heard Mary say, 'Thank you very much.' The door closed and then he heard her whoop with joy. 'I've won! Michael. I've won,' she dashed through to the kitchen tearing into a colourful overprinted envelope.

'What's that?' he said turning away from the cupboard. 'Who was that?'

'John from next door,' she said. 'Just got in from work and found this on his mat. Addressed to me. The postman must have pushed it through the wrong letterbox. I've won fifty thousand,' she said, her face glowing.

Angel looked blank.

She looked at the tonic bottle and then at her husband and said, 'I'll have a gin in it.' She read the letter with shaking hands and then passed it over to Angel. 'Read it. Isn't it wonderful? We can go to Florida this Christmas. I'll have some new curtains in here and in the bedroom. That bathroom needs decorating. We can get a man in to do it. Where's my gin?'

Angel frowned. He'd heard the words, 'Fifty thousand pounds.'

'What is it?' he said.

'It's that quiz, I entered. Don't you remember? I got all the answers correct. It says one hundred per cent. Here. Read it,' she said thrusting it at him impatiently. 'First prize fifty thousand. It's got my name all over it. I'm the winner.'

Angel read it.

Dear Mrs Angel,
This is your lucky day, Mrs Angel of 30 Park Street, Forest Hill Estate, Bromersley!

We are pleased to congratulate you on getting all the questions 100 per cent correct, thereby winning first prize of £50,000 in the all stars' world quiz. The money is yours. The cheque is already made out to you, Mrs Angel.

All you have to do to release the payment is to send your cheque for £124.75 made out to 'The Paymaster' at quiz headquarters in Nigeria, at the box number at the head of this letter. This is to pay the foreign bank their charge for the difference in the exchange rate between euros and sterling to permit the company trustees to release your cheque of £50,000 in sterling payable to Mary Angel through any British bank you wish to designate.

Congratulations, Mrs Angel. You are a winner! We look forward to you claiming your prize money.

'Isn't it wonderful?' Mary said, as she took a swig from her glass.

Angel shoved the letter into her hand, sniffed and said, 'You'd better read it again, then tell them to deduct the hundred and twenty-four pounds from the fifty thousand and send you the difference!'

THE END

OTHER BOOKS BY ROGER SILVERWOOD

YORKSHIRE MURDER MYSTERIES

Book 1: THE MISSING NURSE
Book 2: THE MISSING WIFE
Book 3: THE MAN IN THE PINK SUIT
Book 4: THE MORALS OF A MURDERER
Book 5: THE AUCTION MURDERS
Book 6: THE MISSING KILLER
Book 7: THE UMBRELLA MURDERS
Book 8: THE MISSING MILLIONAIRE
Book 9: THE MISSING THIEF
Book 10: FIND THE LADY
Book 11: THE MISSING MODEL
Book 12: MURDER IN BARE FEET